166

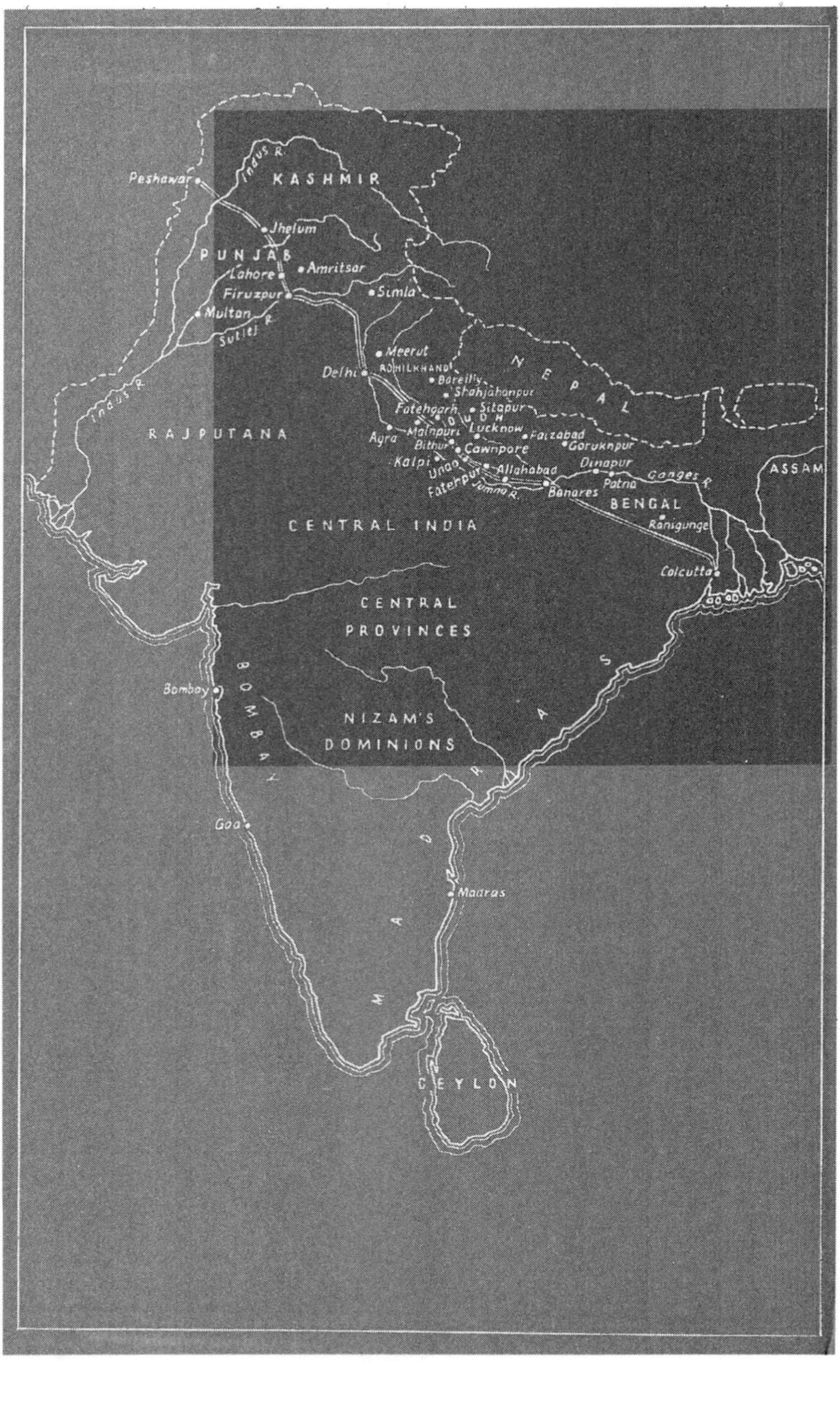
KASHMIR
Indus R.
Peshawar
Jhelum
PUNJAB
Amritsar
Lahore
Firuzpur
Simla
Multan
Sutlej R.
Meerut
ROHILKHAND
Delhi
NEPAL
Bareilly
Shahjahanpur
Indus R.
Fatehgarh
Sitapur
OUDH
RAJPUTANA
Agra
Mainpuri
Lucknow
Faizabad
Gorukhpur
Bithur
Cawnpore
Kalpi
Unao
Allahabad
Dinapur
Fatehpur
Jumna R.
Benares
Patna
Ganges R.
ASSAM
BENGAL
Ranigunge
CENTRAL INDIA
Calcutta
CENTRAL PROVINCES
BOMBAY
Bombay
NIZAM'S DOMINIONS
MADRAS
Goa
Madras
CEYLON

The 93rd Regiment, Highlanders

William Forbes-Mitchell

THE RELIEF OF

LUCKNOW

Edited with an introduction by
Michael Edwardes

THE FOLIO SOCIETY
London 1962

CONTENTS

ILLUSTRATIONS

INTRODUCTION

On Sunday evening, 10th May 1857, three Indian regiments stationed in the town of Meerut—some forty miles north-east of Delhi—shot their officers, broke open the jail and released eighty-five of their comrades who, the day before, had been sentenced to ten years' imprisonment for disobeying the lawful command of their superior officer, and set off with their arms along the road to Delhi. No attempt was made to stop them. The general commanding the station was old, with the chronic indecisiveness of the old, and although he had two British regiments and some artillery at hand he preferred to do nothing. In the meanwhile, the town was given up to looting and rapine.

Next morning, the first of the mutineers reached Delhi. Some went to the palace of Bahadur Shah, titular king of Delhi—the last sad remnant of the once powerful Mughal Empire—and proclaimed him emperor of Hindustan. Others joined their fellows in the three native regiments stationed in Delhi, and persuaded them to kill their officers and then to hunt to death the Europeans in the city. A last message went out on the telegraph line: 'The sepoys have come in from Meerut and are burning everything. Mr Todd is dead and we hear several Europeans . . . We must shut up.' Delhi was in the hands of five thousand rebel soldiers; the English who had survived the massacre fled the city. The Indian Mutiny had begun.

The effect of the mutineers' capture of Delhi was profound. Still looked to in northern India as the real centre of power, the old imperial capital, with its shadowy court and its aged king who composed elegant Urdu poetry, seemed overnight to have come out of its long sleep. A Mughal emperor once again ruled in Delhi. No longer was he a pensioner of the accursed British. The old order was to be restored and the foreigner driven into the sea.

For about three weeks, the British, reeling with the unexpectedness of the revolt, were to have a short respite. Fortunately, the Sikhs of the Punjab—which had been annexed in a bloody war only nine years previously—stood fast, and the British were able to gather their scattered wits and begin to organise a reprisal. Delhi, everyone agreed, must be recaptured quickly, if only for symbolic

reasons. Unluckily, the commander-in-chief was short of transport
and supplies and before he could move further outbreaks had taken
place in Oudh, Rohilkhand, and many parts of Central India. In
almost every case, the sepoys set off towards Delhi after murdering
their officers. In Oudh, however, the mutineers turned back to
besiege the British in Lucknow, where the chief commissioner,
Sir Henry Lawrence, had—with a foresight uncharacteristic of his
colleagues elsewhere—fortified the Residency to withstand a siege.

Meanwhile, the British had slowly begun to move on Delhi.
On 27th May, the commander-in-chief died of cholera at Karnal,
about a hundred miles from his objective. His successor was joined
by Archdale Wilson, formerly second in command at Meerut, and
together they defeated the mutineers at the battle of Badli Sarai
on 8th June and made their camp on the ridge facing the city of
Delhi. Their force numbered under five thousand and the defenders
of the city had about thirty thousand men, an army which increased
daily as mutineers flocked in. All through June and July, in the
most gruelling heat, the little British force clung to the Ridge
under constant attack by the mutineers.

In the Punjab, John Lawrence—the chief commissioner, and
brother of Henry—took the calculated risk of sending troops from
the Punjab to the aid of the British on the Ridge; at the end of
July, John Nicholson and his 'movable' column arrived to reinforce the troops outside Delhi. The British had once again lost
their commander-in-chief, who had died on 5th July. His successor
resigned because of illness. The new commander, Archdale Wilson,
was weak and indecisive and became merely a figure-head.
Nicholson was the real leader.

On 6th September, a heavy siege-train of artillery arrived. On
14th September, the Kashmir gate of the city was blown in and the
city stormed. After six days of bloody fighting, Delhi fell to the
British, and the old king was captured.

While the British had been hanging on to the Ridge, the
rebellion in Oudh centred around Cawnpore and Lucknow. At
Cawnpore, General Wheeler had chosen to occupy an indefensible
entrenchment, but had managed to hold it for twenty days, from
6th to 26th June. In Lucknow, the garrison in the Residency—some
eighteen hundred including women and children—were besieged
by over twenty thousand mutineers, but they held out from 1st
July until the final relief by British troops in November. Great

efforts were made to relieve these two towns. Around them, there took place the fiercest fighting of the whole campaign. On 11th June, the British retook the town of Allahabad. On 7th July, a force of two thousand men commanded by Sir Henry Havelock marched out to reconquer Oudh. This force was decimated by cholera and dysentery. The sun, too, was Havelock's enemy. Nevertheless, outnumbered ten to one, Havelock fought twelve bloody battles between July and September—and won. On 17th July, Cawnpore was retaken. Eight days later, Havelock and his tiny force set out to cover the forty-two miles that separated them from the besieged garrison at Lucknow. After winning two pitched battles, Havelock's men were shattered by cholera and sunstroke and he was forced to fall back on Cawnpore. There, still undaunted, he defeated a large force of mutineers who were attempting to recapture the city. After regaining his strength, Havelock set out once more, on 19th September, to relieve the garrison in the Lucknow Residency. Despite his gallant fighting, another commander—Sir James Outram—had been sent out to supersede Havelock, but Outram volunteered to serve under him until Lucknow was relieved. After three more battles, Havelock fought his way into the Residency at Lucknow on 25th September, five days after the British had recaptured Delhi. These two events marked the turning-point in the Mutiny, although much and bitter fighting was still to come.

Once inside Lucknow, Havelock and Outram were not strong enough to break out again and were themselves besieged. But reinforcements were continually arriving in India from England. With them came two generals who were to bring about the end of the campaign—Sir Colin Campbell (afterwards Lord Clyde) and Sir Hugh Rose.

On 9th November, Sir Colin Campbell advanced with five thousand men upon Lucknow, entering the city on the 16th. The Residency was then evacuated as was the city, and Campbell left Outram and Havelock with some four thousand men in the Alam Bagh, a walled park about four miles from the city. There Havelock died on 24th November. Campbell returned to Cawnpore just in time to defeat the Gwalior contingent of mutineers, around twenty thousand strong, and led by the best of the rebel commanders, Tantia Topi. General Wyndham, who had been left in command at Cawnpore, had been repulsed by this force.

In early December, Campbell proceeded to the reconquest of Oudh. Before Lucknow, he was joined by a force of Gurkhas commanded by Jang Bahadur, who had been sent by the Raja of Nepal to assist the British. Lucknow was finally captured on 1st March 1858. Because Campbell had so few men, he tried in every way to avoid unnecessary skirmishes. Large bodies of mutineers therefore escaped capture and the campaign was prolonged. It was not until May that Bareilly, in Rohilkhand, was captured and large-scale operations in the north brought to an end.

While Campbell was engaged in Oudh, Sir Hugh Rose—starting from Bombay—waged a campaign against the mutineers in Central India. With Mhow as his base, he captured Ratgarh in January 1858 and, after defeating a large army under Tantia Topi at the battle of Betwa in March, stormed the fortress of Jhansi. In May, the campaign seemed to be over. But this was not so. The Rani of Jhansi and Tantia Topi made a sudden move towards Gwalior. There, the ruler was loyal to the British and marched out against them. But his whole army deserted and he himself barely managed to escape to Agra. The rebels occupied Gwalior.

Rose and his weary troops again moved into battle and defeated the rebels in two engagements, in one of which the Rani of Jhansi, dressed as a man, is believed to have been killed. Gwalior was recaptured on 20th June.

Though the rebellion still flickered in scattered places, the Governor-General, Lord Canning, declared it over on 8th July 1858. Some of the rebel leaders escaped, including Tantia Topi, but he was finally betrayed to the British and hanged in April 1859. The old king, Bahadur Shah, was tried, and he died in exile at Rangoon.

The Mutiny was at an end. Perhaps the principal casualty was the East India Company who, starting as traders, had come to be the rulers of India. On 1st November 1858, by proclamation of Queen Victoria, the British Crown assumed the government of India and a new era began.

These are the bare facts, a chronology of battles which leaves a thousand questions unanswered. Only some of them can be dealt with here. The causes of the Mutiny were complex. There had been other mutinies in the East India Company's army. In 1806, sepoys had rebelled at Vellore in Madras province, because they

View of Cawnpore from the river

aggrieved; some were already conspiring against the British before
the Mutiny broke out. Chief among the conspirators were Ahmad
Ullah, 'the Maulvi of Faizabad', advisor to the ex-king of Oudh
who had been dethroned and his state annexed in 1856; Dandu
Pant, called the 'Nana Sahib', the adopted son of a former ruler
whose pension the British had refused to pass on to the Nana
Sahib; and the Rani of Jhansi, whose state had been annexed in
1854. But it was the sepoys who gave the lead and, without them,
it is unlikely that the others would have broken into armed
revolt.

The Mutiny was almost completely confined to soldiers of the
Bengal army. At that time, each of the three 'presidencies' into
which British India was divided—Bengal, Madras and Bombay—
had its own army. The Bengal army was not, in fact, recruited in
Bengal, but further west. Many of the sepoys had their homes in
Oudh, an area which was already seething with discontent over the
deposition of its king and annexation by the British. Many of the
sepoys were of high caste and, therefore, particularly fearful of the
supposed Christianising enthusiasm of the British. By the end of
1856 unrest was rife and the sepoys sullen and insubordinate. They
were encouraged by the knowledge that there were very few
British troops stationed in India—only about forty-five thousand—
while their own strength was nearly a quarter of a million. In
Oudh, there was not one British unit. At Delhi, where the king still
commanded some five thousand retainers, a great ammunition
dump was 'guarded' by two officers and six British sergeants.

All that was needed was a spark to set off the explosion. Ironic-
ally, perhaps, it came from the introduction of a new rifle with a
special type of cartridge. 'A consciousness of power', wrote the
Commissioner of Meerut after the outbreak, 'had grown up in the
army which could only be exorcised by mutiny, and the cry of
the cartridge brought the latent spirit of revolt into action.' If
there had been no cartridge, some other excuse would have been
found.

The new Enfield rifle was supplied with a cartridge which had a
protective covering of grease. To load the rifle, it was necessary
to bite the end off the cartridge. Soon the rumour grew that the
grease was made from beef fat or hog's lard, and that an attempt
was being made deliberately to break the caste of the Hindus and
to insult the religious prejudices of the Muslims. The cow is sacred

to Hindus, and the pig is an unclean animal to Muslims. Regiments began to refuse to obey their officers.

The first outbreak came in the 34th Native Infantry. A sepoy who was under the influence of opium—and convinced that the English were about to destroy the sepoys—shot the adjutant of his regiment and encouraged others to attack the English sergeant-major. The sepoy's name was Mangal Pandy. From firing the first shot of the Mutiny, he achieved the notoriety of providing the nickname which English soldiers gave to the mutineers—'pandies'. In April, native infantry at Meerut refused to use the new cartridges. Punishment was harsh and, as we have seen, provoked the sepoys into mutinying on 10th May.

From that date onwards, the war was carried on with sometimes bestial ferocity on both sides. Crazy with fear, the sepoys murdered English women and children, and the British retaliated with lynchings and village-burnings which made no discrimination between the guilty and the innocent. By 20th June, J. W. Kaye—the historian of the Mutiny—records: 'Soldiers and civilians alike were holding Bloody Assize, or slaying natives without any assize at all, regardless of sex or age . . . Volunteer hanging parties went into the districts and amateur executioners were not wanting to the occasion. One gentleman boasted of the numbers he had finished off quite "in an artistic manner", with mango trees for gibbets and elephants for drops, the victims of this wild justice being strung up, as though for pastime, in the form of figures of eight.' Violence and cruelty bred further violence and cruelty. The sepoys had no inducement to show mercy since they received none, and even women had no value as hostages.

The racial hatreds produced by the Mutiny were never forgotten by either side. In a profound sense, the two peoples—British and Indian—could never trust each other again until, in 1947, by her abdication of power, Britain healed the wounds of nearly a century before.

The events of the Mutiny produced their quota of heroes in both camps. On the British side, there was John Nicholson, 'the hero of Delhi'. There was Lieutenant Hodson, the scallywag guerilla fighter who personally shot two of the Mughal princes in Delhi when he believed they were about to be released by the mob, and who met his death at the relief of Lucknow—where he had joined in the assault for the fun of the thing. Also at Lucknow was the

first civilian V.C., T. H. Kavanagh, who slipped out of the besieged
Residency disguised as a native to guide the relieving force under
Sir Colin Campbell through the narrow streets of the city. There
were many more, unsung and forgotten. On the rebel side there
were Tantia Topi, the best of the rebel commanders, who was
finally betrayed by a friend; the Rani of Jhansi, like some Indian
Boadicea, fighting as a soldier with her men; and Hazrat Mahal
(one of the queens of the ex-king of Oudh), who escaped the
vengeance of the British and died in Nepal in 1874.

Both sides, too, had their dark and sinister figures. The infamous
Nana Sahib of Cawnpore is familiar to every schoolboy. After
destroying the remnants of the garrison of Cawnpore, in spite of
having guaranteed them a safe conduct, he shut up the women and
children in part of his palace until, on the approach of Havelock's
force, he allowed his retainers to murder two hundred and eleven
of them and throw their bodies down a well. This single episode
inspired the savage reprisals of the British soldiers who were taken
to the scene of the massacre, where—*after* the British had recaptured the town—someone had scrawled harrowing phrases on the
walls. Cawnpore was to suffer a second massacre, for Colonel
Neill then issued an order that every captured rebel, proved or not,
'will be taken down to the house [where the women and children
were killed] and will be forced to clean up a small portion of the
bloodstains, the task will be made as revolting to his feelings as
possible . . . After properly cleaning up his portion, the culprit
will be immediately hanged'. The guilty men, of course, had fled
long before Neill arrived, but that did not deter him from carrying
out his nauseating plan.

With these examples—and many others—before him, there is
little wonder that the British soldier behaved callously towards the
enemy, though, as always, there were many episodes of genuine
kindness and even of compassion, as the writer of the following
reminiscences records.

Forbes-Mitchell's account is a 'voice from the ranks', a view of the
campaign from below stairs. Most memoirs of the Mutiny were
written by officers or civil officials anxious to justify their own
position or to protect that of others. Forbes-Mitchell—an articu-
late, intelligent and canny sergeant in the 93rd Sutherland Highlanders—saw a great deal more than his position might have

warranted. He had no axe to grind and no reputation to consider. He therefore told the truth as he saw it, remarkably free from bias and, for his time, from the fashionable cant.

His memoirs were not published until 1893, under the title of *Reminiscences of the Great Mutiny*, and he no doubt took the opportunity of exercising hindsight and polishing a few of his memories. But his words still have the fresh smell of immediacy, and he certainly made no attempt to dramatise his story. In fact, his book is badly organised and the chronology is a little out of order. In editing the work, I have therefore cut a few tiresome diversions and rearranged some passages so that the narrative proceeds in more comprehensible phases. I have added to the author's own footnotes, and my additions are marked [M.E.] to distinguish them from Forbes-Mitchell's.

Most of Forbes-Mitchell's story deals with the campaign in Oudh and it has, as its highlights, the second relief of the Residency at Lucknow and the final capture of the city. In between are the sorrows, the miseries, the hell of a soldier's life in the heat of the Indian summer. All the horror and the anguish of those terrible times are summed up in the words of this dry and observant Scotsman, whose occasional touches of wry humour, slightly maudlin sentimentality, and brisk no-nonsense appreciation, bring alive an almost forgotten episode in British imperial history with a reality which more weighty historical works can never achieve.

MICHAEL EDWARDES

THE RELIEF OF LUCKNOW

1. ARRIVAL IN INDIA

ON the return of the Ninety-Third [Sutherland Highlanders] from the Crimea they were quartered at Dover, and, in April 1857, the regiment was detailed for the expedition forming for China under Lord Elgin, and all time-expired men and those unfit for foreign service were carefully weeded from the service companies and formed into a depot. The ten service companies were recruited by volunteers from the other Highland regiments, the Forty-Second, Seventy-Second, Seventy-Ninth, and Ninety-Second, each giving a certain number of men, bringing the Ninety-Third up to a corps of eleven hundred bayonets. About the 20th of May the Ninety-Third left Dover for Portsmouth, where we were reviewed by the Queen accompanied by Sir Colin Campbell, who took final leave, as he then supposed, of the regiment which had stood with him in the 'thin red line' of Balaklava against the terrible Cossacks. On the first of June three companies, of which mine formed one, embarked in a coasting steamer for Plymouth, where we joined the *Belleisle*, an old 84-gun two-decker, which had been converted into a transport for the China expedition. This detachment of the Ninety-Third was under the command of Colonel the Honourable Adrian Hope, and the captains of the three companies were Cornwall, Dawson, and Williams—my company being that of Captain E. S. F. G. Dawson, an officer of great experience, who had served in another regiment (I forget which) throughout the Kaffir war in the Cape, and was adjutant of the Ninety-Third at the Alma, where he had his horse shot under him. The remaining seven companies, forming headquarters under Colonel A. S. Leith-Hay, sailed from Portsmouth in the steam transport *Mauritius* about ten days after us.

Although an old wooden ship, the *Belleisle* was a very comfortable transport and a good sailer, and we sighted land at the Cape on the morning of the 9th of August, having called and posted mails at both Madeira and the Cape Verde Islands on our way. We were at anchor in Simon's Bay by the afternoon of the 9th of August, where we heard the first news of the Indian Mutiny, and

that our destination was changed from China to Calcutta; and
during the 10th and 11th all was bustle, tightening up rigging,
taking in fuel for cooking, and refilling our empty water-tanks.
On the evening of the 11th, just as it was becoming dark, a steamer
came up the bay, and anchored quite close to the *Belleisle*; and on
our bugler's sounding the regimental call, it turned out to be the
Mauritius with headquarters on board. Most of our officers immediately went on board, and many of the men in the three companies
were gratified by receiving letters from parents, sweethearts, and
friends, which had reached Portsmouth after our detachment had
left. On the forenoon of the 12th of August the *Belleisle* left
Simon's Bay, making all sail day and night for Calcutta. The ship's
crew numbered nine hundred men, being made up of drafts for the
ships of the China squadron. Every yard of canvas that the masts
or spars could carry was crowded on day and night; and we reached
the pilot station at the Sandheads on the 19th of September, thirty-
eight days from the Cape, where we learned that the *Mauritius*,
with our headquarters, had just proceeded up the river.

Early on the 20th, the anniversary of the Alma, we got tug
steamers and proceeded up the Hugli anchoring off the steps at
Prinsep's *ghat** on the afternoon of the 21st of September. Our
progress up the river was all excitement. We had two tug
steamers, the *Belleisle* being considered too large for a single tug;
and the pilot and tug commanders all sent bundles of the latest
Calcutta papers on board, from which we learned the first news of
the sieges of Delhi and Lucknow, of the horrible massacre at
Cawnpore, and of the gallant advance of the small force under
Generals Havelock, Neill, and Outram for the relief of Lucknow.
When passing Garden Reach, every balcony, verandah, and house-
top was crowded with ladies and gentlemen waving their hand-
kerchiefs and cheering us, all our men being in full Highland dress
and the pipers playing on the poop. In passing No. 46 Garden
Reach the flood-tide was still running up too strong for the *Belleisle*
to come into harbour, and we anchored for about an hour just
opposite No. 46. The house and steps of the *ghat* were crowded
with ladies and gentlemen cheering us; and one of my comrades,
a young man named Frank Henderson, said to me, 'Forbes-
Mitchell, how would you like to be owner of a palace like that?'
when I, on the spur of the moment, without any thought, replied,

* A landing-place.

'I'll be master of that house and garden yet before I leave India.'*
Poor Henderson replied: 'I firmly believe you will, if you make up
your mind for it; but as for myself, I feel that I shall either die or
be killed in this war. I am convinced I shall never see the end of it.
I have dreamed of my dead father every night since we sighted the
pilot-brig, and I know my days are numbered. But as for you—I
have also dreamed of you, and I am sure you will go safely through
the war, and live for many years, and become a prosperous man in
India. Mark my words; I am convinced of it.' We had a Church of
England chaplain on the *Belleisle*, and service every morning, and
Henderson and myself, with many others, formed part of the
chaplain's Sunday and Wednesday evening prayer-meeting class.
'Since ever we sighted the pilot-brig,' Henderson went on to say,
'and my dead father has commenced to appear to me in my dreams,
I have felt every day at morning prayers that the words, "That
we may return in safety to enjoy the blessings of the land, with the
fruits of our labours, and with a thankful remembrance of Thy
mercies, to praise and glorify Thy holy name, through Jesus Christ
our Lord," had no reference to me, and I cannot join in them. But
when the chaplain read the prayers this morning he looked straight
at you when he pronounced that part of the prayer, and I felt that
the blessing prayed for rests on you. Mark my words, and remember them when I am dead and buried.' Strange to say, on the 16th
of November Henderson was severely wounded at the taking of
the Shah Najaf, died in the retreat from Lucknow on the evening of
the 20th of November, and was buried on the banks of the Ganges,
just opposite the bridge of boats at Cawnpore.

The arrival of the Ninety-Third caused quite a sensation in
Calcutta, where but few Highland regiments had ever been seen
before. To quote the words of an eye-witness writing from Calcutta to friends at home, and published in the Aberdeen *Herald*,
describing a party of the Ninety-Third which was sent ashore to
store the heavy baggage which had to be left in Calcutta: 'On
hearing the Ninety-Third in the streets, Scotchmen who had long
been exiled from home rose from their desks, rushed out, and stood
at the doors of their offices, looking with feelings of pride at their
stalwart countrymen, and listening with smiles of pleasure to the
sounds of their own northern tongue, long unfamiliar to their ears.

* He was. In fact, he established the Bon Accord Rope Works there in 1889.
[M.E.]

Many brought out tankards of cool beer, and invited the men as they passed along to drink, and the Highlanders required but little pressing, for the sun was hot, and, to use their own vernacular, the exercise made them *gey an' drouthy.'*

* 'Good and thirsty.' [M.E.]

2. CAWNPORE AFTER THE MASSACRE

BY the 25th of September the whole of the Ninety-Third were once more together in Chinsurah, and on the 28th the first company, the Grenadiers under Captain Middleton, started by rail for Ranigunge *en route* for Lucknow, and a company followed daily in regular rotation till the light company left Chinsurah on the 7th of October. From Ranigunge to Benares the old bullock-train was arranged with relays of bullocks from eight to ten miles apart, according to the nature of the road, and six men were told off to each cart to ride and march by relief. Thus we proceeded, making an average advance of from twenty-five to thirty miles daily, halting every day about ten o'clock for cooking, resuming our march about four o'clock, and so on through the night for coolness; the bullocks did not average more than two and a half miles per hour, and there was always considerable delay at the different stations, changing teams. In this way my company reached Benares on the 17th of October. From Benares we proceeded by detachments of two or three companies to Allahabad; the country between Benares and Allahabad, being overrun by different bands of mutineers, was too dangerous for small detachments of one company. My company reached Allahabad on the 19th of October. There we were supplied with the usual Indian field equipment of tents, etc. By this time the railway had been pushed on in the direction of Cawnpore to a place called Lohunga, about forty-eight miles from Allahabad, but no stations were built. On the 22nd of October my company, with three others, left Allahabad, packed into open trucks or wagons used by the railway contractors for the construction of the line. From Lohunga we commenced our daily marches on foot, with our tents on elephants, *en route* for Cawnpore.

By this time a considerable force had assembled at Allahabad, consisting of artillery from the Cape, Peel's Naval Brigade, detachments of the Fifth Fusiliers, the Fifty-Third, and Ninetieth Light Infantry. But the only complete regiment was the Ninety-Third Highlanders, over a thousand men, in splendid condition, armed with the Enfield rifle, and, what was of more importance, well drilled to the use of it.*

After leaving Lohunga, the first place of note which we reached was Fatehpur, seventy-two miles from Allahabad. At Fatehpur I met some native Christians whom I had first seen in Allahabad, and who were, or had been, connected with mission work, and could speak English. They had returned from Allahabad to look after property which they had been obliged to abandon when they fled from Fatehpur on the outbreak of the Mutiny. These men all knew Dr Duff,† or had heard of him, and were most anxious to talk to Dr Duff's countrymen, as they called the Highlanders.

When the detachment of which my company formed part marched through Fatehpur, it was rumoured that the Banda and Dinapur mutineers, joined by large bodies of *badmashes*,‡ numbering over ten thousand men, with three batteries of regular artillery mustering eighteen guns, had crossed the Jumna, and were threatening our communications with Allahabad. Owing to this report, No. 2, or Captain Cornwallis's company of the Ninety-Third, was left in the fort at Fatehpur to guard provisions, etc., as that post had been greatly strengthened by a party of sappers and was formed into a depot for commissariat stores and ammunition, which were being pushed on by every available mode of conveyance from Allahabad. We left Fatehpur on the 25th of October, and arrived at Cawnpore on the morning of the 27th, having marched the forty-six miles in two days.

When we reached Cawnpore we found everything quiet, and Brigadier Wilson, of the Sixty-Fourth Regiment, in command. Wheeler's immortal entrenchment was deserted, but a much stronger one had lately been built, or rather was still under construction on the right (the Cawnpore) bank of the Ganges, to protect the bridge of boats crossing into Oudh. This place was constructed of strong and well-planned earthworks, and every available coolie in Cawnpore was at work, from daylight till dark, strengthening the place. Bastions and ramparts were being constructed of every conceivable material, besides the usual gabions and fascines. Bales of cotton were built into the ramparts, bags of

* See Introduction, p. 10. [M.E.]
† Dr Alexander Duff, the missionary who in 1845 founded the Scottish Churches College in Calcutta. [M.E.]
‡ Bad characters, scoundrels.

every size and shape, soldiers' knapsacks, etc., were filled with earth; in brief, everything that could possibly hold a few spadefuls of earth, and could thereby assist in raising a defensive breastwork, had been appropriated for building the parapet-walls, and a ditch of considerable depth and width was being excavated.

The day before we reached Cawnpore, a strong column from Delhi had arrived under command of Sir Hope Grant, and was encamped on the plain. The detachment of the Ninety-Third did not pitch tents, but was accommodated in some buildings, on which the roofs were still left, near General Wheeler's entrenchment. My company occupied the dak* bungalow.

After a few hours' rest, we were allowed to go out in parties of ten or twelve to visit the horrid scene of the recent treachery and massacre. The first place my party reached was General Wheeler's so-called entrenchment, the ramparts of which at the highest places did not exceed four feet, and were so thin that at the top they could never have been bullet-proof! The entrenchment and the barracks inside of it were complete ruins, and the only wonder about it was how the small force could have held out so long. In the rooms of the building were still lying strewn about the remains of articles of women's and children's clothing, broken toys, torn pictures, books, pieces of music, etc. Among the books, I picked up a New Testament in Gaelic, but without any name on it. All the blank leaves had been torn out, and at the time I formed the opinion that they had been used for gun-waddings, because, close beside the Testament, there was a broken single-barrelled duck gun, which had evidently been smashed by a 9-pounder shot lying near. I annexed the Testament as a relic. The Psalms and Paraphrases in Gaelic verses are complete, but the first chapter of Matthew and up to the middle of the seventh verse of the second chapter are wanting. The Testament must have belonged to some Scotch Highlander in the garrison.

From the entrenchment we went to the Suttee Chowra *ghat*, where the doomed garrison were permitted to embark in the boats in which they were murdered, and traces of the treachery were still very plain, many skeletons, etc., lying about unburied among the bushes.

We then went to see the slaughter-house in which the unfortunate women and children had been barbarously murdered, and the

* Travellers'. [M.E.]

well into which their mangled bodies were afterwards flung. Our guide was a native of the ordinary camp-follower class, who could speak intelligible barrack-room English. He told us that he had been born in a battery of European artillery, in which his fore-fathers had been shoeblacks for unknown generations, and his name, he stated, was 'Peshawarie,' because he had been born in Peshawar, when the English occupied it during the first advance to Kabul. His apparent age coincided with this statement. He claimed to have been in Sir Hugh Wheeler's entrenchment with the artillery all the time of the siege, and to have had a narrow escape of his life at the last. He told us a story which I have never seen mentioned elsewhere, that the Nana Sahib, through a spy, tried to bribe the commissariat bakers who had remained with the English to put arsenic into the bread, which they refused to do, and that after the massacre of the English at the *ghat* the Nana had these bakers taken and put alive into their own ovens, and there cooked and thrown to the pigs. These bakers were Muhammadans. Of course, I had no means of testing the truth of this statement. Our guide showed no desire to minimise the horrors of the massacre and the murders to which he said he had been an eye-witness. However, from the traces, still too apparent, the bare facts, without exaggeration, must have been horrible enough. But with reference to the women and children, from the cross-questions I put to our guide, I then formed the opinion, which I have never since altered, that most of the European women had been most barbarously murdered, but not dishonoured, with the exception of a few of the young and good-looking ones, who, our guide stated, were forcibly carried off to become Muhammadans.* But I need not dwell on these points.

Most of the men of my company visited the slaughter-house and well, and what we there saw was enough to fill our hearts with feelings which I need not here dwell on; it was long before those feelings could be controlled. On the date of my visit a great part of the house had not been cleaned out; the floors of the rooms were still covered with congealed blood, littered with trampled, torn dresses of women and children, shoes, slippers, and locks of long hair, many of which had evidently been severed from the living scalps by sword-cuts. But among the traces of barbarous torture

---

* This is untrue. Only one, the Eurasian daughter of General Wheeler, was abducted, and after the Mutiny she refused to leave her Muslim husband. See p. 114. [M.E.]

and cruelty which excited horror and a desire for revenge, one stood out prominently beyond all others. It was an iron hook fixed into the wall of one of the rooms in the house, about six feet from the floor. I could not possibly say for what purpose this hook had originally been fixed in the wall. I examined it carefully, and it appeared to have been an old fixture, which had been seized on as a diabolic and convenient instrument of torture by the inhuman wretches engaged in murdering the women and children. This hook was covered with dried blood, and from the marks on the whitewashed wall, it was evident that a little child had been hung on to it by the neck with its face to the wall, where the poor thing must have struggled for long, perhaps in the sight of its helpless mother, because the wall all round the hook on a level with it was covered with the hand-prints, and below the hook with the foot-prints, in blood, of a little child.

At the time of my visit the well was only about half-filled in, and the bodies of the victims only partially covered with earth. A gallows, with three or four ropes ready attached, stood facing the slaughter-house, half-way between it and the well; and during my stay three wretches were hanged, after having been flogged, and each made to clean about a square foot of the blood from the floor of the house. Our guide told us that these men had only been captured the day before, tried that morning, and found guilty as having assisted at the massacre.

During our visit a party of officers came to the slaughter-house, among whom was Dr Munro, Surgeon of the Ninety-Third. When I saw him he was examining the hook covered with dried blood, and the hand and foot-prints of the child on the wall, with tears streaming down his cheeks. He was a most kind-hearted man, and I remember, when he came out of the house, that he cast a look of pity on the three wretches about to be hanged, and I overheard him say to another officer who was with him: 'This is horrible and unchristian to look at; but I do hope those are the same wretches who tortured the little child on the hook inside that room.' At this time there was no writing either in pencil or charcoal on the walls of the slaughter-house.* I am positive on this point, because I looked for any writing. There was writing on the walls of the barracks inside General Wheeler's entrenchment, but not on the walls of the slaughter-house, though they were much splashed with

* See Introduction, p. 12. [M.E.]

blood and slashed with sword-cuts, where blows aimed at the victims had evidently been dodged and the swords had struck the walls. Such marks were most numerous in the corners of the rooms. The number of victims butchered in the house, counted and buried in the well by General Havelock's force, was one hundred and eighteen women and ninety-two children.

Up to the date of my visit, a brigade-order, issued by Brigadier-General J. G. S. Neill, First Madras Fusiliers, was still in force. This order bears date the 25th of July, 1857. Its purport was to this effect: That, after trial and condemnation, all prisoners found guilty of having taken part in the murder of the European women and children, were to be taken into the slaughter-house by Major Bruce's *mehtar** police, and there made to crouch down, and with their mouths lick clean a square foot of the blood-soaked floor before being taken to the gallows and hanged. This order was carried out in my presence as regards the three wretches who were hanged that morning. The dried blood on the floor was first moistened with water, and the lash of the warder was applied till the wretches kneeled down and cleaned their square foot of flooring. This order remained in force till the arrival of Sir Colin Campbell in Cawnpore on the 3rd of November, 1857, when he promptly put a stop to it as unworthy of the English name and a Christian Government.

General Hope Grant's brigade and part of the Ninety-Third Highlanders crossed the bridge of boats at Cawnpore, and entered Oudh on the 30th of October, with a convoy of provisions and ammunition *en route* to Lucknow. My company, with three others remained in Cawnpore three days longer, and crossed into Oudh on the 2nd of November, encamping a short distance from the bridge of boats.

On the morning of the 3rd a salute was fired from the mud fort on the Cawnpore side, from which we learned, to the great delight of the Ninety-Third, that Sir Colin Campbell had come up from Calcutta. Shortly after the salute some of our officers joined us from the Cawnpore side, and gave us the news, which had been brought by the Commander-in-Chief, that a few days before three companies of the Fifty-Third and Captain Cornwallis's company, No. 2, of the Ninety-Third, which had been left at Fatehpur, with part of the Naval Brigade under Captain William Peel, had formed a force

* Sweeper, scavenger; one of the lowest castes.

of about five hundred men under the command of Colonel Powell of the Fifty-Third, marched out from Fatehpur to a place called Khujwah, and attacked and beaten the Banda and Dinapur mutineers, numbering over ten thousand, who had been threatening our communications with Allahabad. The victory for some time had been doubtful, as the mutineers were a well-equipped force, strongly posted and numbering more than twenty to one of the attacking force, possessing moreover, three well-drilled batteries of artillery, comprising eighteen guns. Colonel Powell was killed early in the action, and the command then devolved on Captain Peel of the Naval Brigade. Although hard pressed at first, the force eventually gained a complete and glorious victory, totally routing the rebels, capturing most of their guns, and driving the remnant of them across the Jumna, whence they had come. The company of the Ninety-Third lost heavily, having one officer wounded and sixteen men killed or wounded. The officer, Lieutenant Cunyngham, was reported to have lost a leg, which caused general sorrow and regret throughout the regiment, as he was a most promising young officer and very popular with the men. During the day when more correct and fuller reports came in, we were all very glad to hear that, although severely wounded, the lieutenant had not lost a limb, and that the surgeons considered they would not only be able to save his leg, but that he might be fit to return to duty in a few months, which he eventually did, and was present at the siege of Lucknow.

During the afternoon of the 3rd of November more stores of provisions and ammunition crossed the river with some of Peel's 24-pounder guns, and on the morning of the 4th, long before daylight, we were on the march for Lucknow, under command of Colonel Leith-Hay, leaving Cawnpore and its horrors behind us, but neither forgotten nor disregarded. Every man in the regiment was determined to risk his life to save the women and children in the Residency of Lucknow from a similar fate. None were inclined to pay any heed to the French maxim that *les représailles sont toujours inutiles*, nor inclined to ponder and moralise on the lesson and warning given by the horrible catastrophe which had overtaken our people at Cawnpore. Many too were inclined to blame the Commander-in-Chief for having cancelled the brigade order of General Neill.

3. THE ADVANCE ON LUCKNOW

WHEN proceeding on our march to Lucknow it was clear as noonday to the meanest capacity that we were now in an enemy's country. None of the villages along the route were inhabited, the only visible signs of life about them being a few mangy pariah dogs. The people had all fled on the first advance of Havelock, and had not returned; and it needed no great powers of observation to fully understand that the whole population of Oudh was against us.

The deserted villages gave the country a miserable appearance. Not only were they forsaken, but we found, on reaching our first halting-ground, that the whole of the small bazaar of camp-followers, consisting of goatherds, bread, milk, and butter-sellers, etc., which had accompanied us from Allahabad, had returned to Cawnpore, none daring to accompany the force into Oudh. This was most disappointing for young soldiers with good appetites and sound digestions, who depended on bazaar *chupatties*,* with a *chittack*† of butter and a pint of goat's milk at the end of the march, to eke out the scanty commissariat allowance of rations. What made the privation the more keenly felt, was the custom of serving out at one time three days' biscuits, supposed to run four to the pound, but which, I fear, were often short weight. Speaking for myself, I did not control my appetite, but commenced to eat from my haversack on the march, the whole of my three days' biscuits usually disappearing before we reached the first halting-ground, and believe me, I ran no danger of a fit of indigestion. To demolish twelve ordinary-sized ship's biscuits, during a march of twenty to twenty-five miles, was no great tax on a young and healthy stomach.

I may here remark that my experience is that, after a forced march, it would be far more beneficial to the men if the general commanding were to serve out an extra ration of tea or coffee with a pound of bread or biscuit instead of extra grog. The latter was often issued during the forced marches of the Mutiny, but never an extra ration of food; and my experience is that a pint of good tea is far more refreshing than a dram of rum. Let me also note here

* Unleavened girdle-cakes.　　　　　　　　† Rather less than two ounces.

most emphatically that regimental canteens and the fixed ration of
rum in the field are the bane of the army. At the same time I am
no teetotaller. In addition to the bazaar people, our cooks and
*dhobies** had also deserted. This was not such a serious matter for
the Ninety-Third just fresh from the Crimea, as it was for the old
Indian regiments. Men for cooking were at once told off for each
of our tents; but the cooking-utensils had also gone with the cooks,
or not come on; the rear-guard had seen nothing of them. There
were, however, large copper water-cans attached to each tent,
and these were soon brought into use for cooking, and plenty of
earthen pots were to be found in the deserted houses of the vil-
lagers. Highlanders, and especially Highlanders who are old
campaigners, are not lacking in resources where the preparation
of food is concerned.

I will relate a rather amusing incident which happened to the
men of the colour-sergeant's tent of my company—Colour-
Sergeant David Morton, a Fifeshire man, an old soldier of close on
twenty years' service, one of the old 'unlimited service' men, whose
regimental number was 1100, if I remember rightly. A soldier's
approximate service, I may here state, can almost always be told
from his regimental number, as each man on enlisting takes the
next consecutive number in the regiment, and as these numbers
often range up to 8000 or even 10,000 before commencing again
at No. 1, it is obvious that the earlier numbers indicate the oldest
soldiers. The men in the Ninety-Third with numbers between
1000 and 2000 had been with the regiment in Canada before the
Crimean War, so David Morton, it will be seen, was an old
soldier; but he had never seen tobacco growing in the field, and in
the search for fuel to cook a dinner, he had come across a small plot
of luxuriant tobacco leaf. He came back with an armful of it for
Duncan Mackenzie, who was the improvised cook for the men of
his tent, and told us all that he had secured a rare treat for our
soup, having fallen on a plot of 'real Scotch curly kail'! The men
were all hungry, and the tobacco leaves were soon chopped fine,
washed, and put into the soup. But when that soup was cooked it
was a 'caution'. I was the only non-smoker in the squad, and was
the first to detect that instead of 'real Scotch curly kail' we had got
'death in the pot'! As before remarked we were all hungry, having
marched over twenty miles since we had last tasted food. Although

* Laundry-men.

noticing that there was something wrong about the soup and the 'curly kail', I had swallowed enough to act as a powerful emetic before I was aware of the full extent of the bitter taste. At first we feared it was a deadly poison, and so we were all much relieved when the *bheestie*,* who picked up some of the rejected stalks, assured us that it was only green tobacco which had been cooked in the soup.

The desertion of our camp-followers was significant. An army in India is followed by another army whose general or commander-in-chief is the bazaar *kotwal*.† These people carry all their household goods and families with them, their only houses being their little tents. The elder men, at the time of which I write, could all talk of the victories of Lords Lake and Combermere, and the Kabul war of 1840–42, and the younger hands could tell us of the victories of Lords Gough and Hardinge in the Punjab. The younger generations took up the handicrafts of their fathers, as barbers, cobblers, cooks, shoeblacks, and so forth, a motley hive bred in camps but unwarlike, always in the rear of the army. Most of these camp-followers were low-caste. Hindus, very few of them were Muhammadans, except the *bheesties*. I may remark that the *bheesties* and the *dooly*-bearers‡ (the latter were under the hospital guard) were the only camp-followers who did not desert us when we crossed into Oudh. The natives fully believed that our column was doomed to extermination; there is no doubt that they knew of the powerful force collecting in our rear, consisting of the Gwalior Contingent, which had never yet been beaten and was supposed to be invincible; also of the Central India mutineers who were gathering for a fresh attack on Cawnpore under the leadership of Nana Sahib, Koer Singh, Tantia Topi, and other commanders. But we learned all this afterwards, when this army retook Cawnpore in our rear, which story I will relate in its proper place. For the present, we must resume our advance into Oudh.

Every hour's march brought us three miles nearer Lucknow, and before we made our first halt, we could distinctly hear the guns of the enemy bombarding the Residency. Foot-sore and tired as they were, the report of each salvo made the men step out with a

* The *bheesties*, or water-carriers, have been noted for bravery and fidelity in every Indian campaign.
† The native official in charge of the bazaar; he possessed certain magisterial powers.
‡ A covered litter used for carrying the wounded. [M.E.]

firmer tread and a more determined resolve to overcome all difficulties, and to carry relief to the beleaguered garrison and the
helpless women and children. I may mention that the cowardly
treachery of the enemy, and their barbarous murders of women and
children, had converted the war of the Mutiny into a *guerre à la
mort*—a war of the most cruel and exterminating form, in which
no quarter was given on either side. Up to the final relief of Lucknow and the second capture of Cawnpore, and the total rout of the
Gwalior Contingent on the 6th of December, 1857, it would have
been impossible for the Europeans to have guarded their prisoners,
and, for that reason, it was obvious that prisoners were not to be
taken; while on the part of the rebels, wherever they met a Christian or a white man, he was at once slain without pity or remorse,
and natives who attempted to assist or conceal a distressed
European did so at the risk of their own lives and property. It was
both horrible and demoralising for the army to be engaged in such
a war.

On the 10th of November the total force that could be collected
for the final relief of Lucknow was encamped on the plain about
five miles in front of the Alambagh. The total strength was under
five thousand of all arms, and the only really complete regiment
was the Ninety-Third Highlanders. By this time the whole
regiment, consisting of ten companies, had reached the front,
numbering over a thousand men in the prime of manhood, about
seven hundred of them having the Crimean medals on their breasts.
By the afternoon of the 11th of November, the whole force had
been told off into brigades. The Fifty-Third Shropshire Light
Infantry, the Ninety-Third, and the Fourth Punjab Infantry, just
come down from Delhi with Sir Hope Grant, formed the fourth
brigade, under Colonel the Honourable Adrian Hope of the Ninety-
Third as brigadier. The whole of our regiment were not present.
There were only six or seven companies, and there was no field-
officer, Captain Walton, late commandant of the Calcutta Volunteers, being the senior captain present. Under these circum-
stances Colonel Gordon, of ours, was temporarily put in command
of the Fifty-Third. The whole force was formed up in a line of
Columns on the afternoon of the 11th for the inspection of the
Commander-in-Chief. The Ninety-Third formed the extreme left
of the line in quarter-distance column, in full Highland costume,
with feather bonnets and dark waving plumes, a solid mass of

brawny-limbed men. I have never seen a more magnificent regiment than the Ninety-Third looked that day, and I was proud to have formed one of its units.

The old Chief rode along the line, commencing from the right, halting and addressing a short speech to each corps as he came along. The eyes of the Ninety-Third were eagerly turned towards Sir Colin and his staff as he advanced, the men remarking among themselves that none of the other corps had given him a single cheer, but had taken whatever he had said to them in solemn silence. At last he approached us; we were called to attention, and formed close column, so that every man might hear what was said. When Sir Colin rode up, he appeared to have a worn and haggard expression on his face, but he was received with such a cheer, or rather shout of welcome, as made the echoes ring from the Alambagh and the surrounding woods. His wrinkled brow at once became smooth, and his wearied-looking features broke into a smile, as he acknowledged the cheer by a hearty salute, and addressed us almost exactly as follows. I stood near him and heard every word. 'Ninety-Third! when I took leave of you in Portsmouth, I never thought I should see you again. I expected the bugle, or maybe the bagpipes, to sound a call for me to go somewhere else long before you would be likely to return to our dearly-loved home. But another commander has decreed it otherwise, and here I am prepared to lead you through another campaign. And I must tell you, my lads, there is work of difficulty and danger before us—harder work and greater dangers than any we encountered in the Crimea. But I trust to you to overcome the difficulties and to brave the dangers. The eyes of the people at home—I may say the eyes of Europe and of the whole of Christendom are upon us, and we must relieve our countrymen, women, and children, now shut up in the Residency of Lucknow. The lives at stake are not merely those of soldiers, who might well be expected to cut themselves out, or to die sword in hand. We have to rescue helpless women and children from a fate worse than death. When you meet the enemy, you must remember that he is well armed and well provided with ammunition, and that he can play at long bowls as well as you can, especially from behind loopholed walls. So when we make an attack you must come to close quarters as quickly as possible; keep well together, and use the bayonet. Remember that the cowardly sepoys, who are eager to murder women and children, cannot look

clean off just level with his ears. He fell just in front of me, and I had to step over his body before a single drop of blood had had time to flow. The colour-sergeant of his company turned to me and said, 'Poor lad! how can I tell his poor mother. What would she think if she were to see him now! He was her favourite laddie!' There was no leisure for moralising, however; we were completely within the range of the enemy's guns, and the next shot cut down seven or eight of the light company, and old Colonel Leith-Hay was calling out, 'Keep steady, men; close up the ranks, and don't waver in face of a battery manned by cowardly Asiatics.' The shots were now coming thick, bounding along the hard ground, and MacBean, the adjutant, was behind the line telling the men in an undertone, 'Don't mind the colonel; open out and let them (the round-shot) through, keep plenty of room and watch the shot.' By this time the staff-officer, whose horse only had been killed under him, had got clear of the carcase, and the Ninety-Third, seeing him on his feet again, gave him a rousing cheer. He was soon in the saddle of a spare horse, and the artillery dashed to the front under his direction, taking the guns of the enemy in flank. The sepoys bolted down the hill for shelter in the Martinière, while our little force took possession of the Dilkusha palace. The Ninety-Third had lost ten men killed and wounded by the time we had driven the enemy and their guns through the long grass into the entrenchments in front of the Martinière. I may note here that there were very few trees on the Dilkusha heights at this time, and between the heights and the city there was a bare plain, so that signals could be passed between us and the Residency. A semaphore was erected on the top of the palace as soon as it was taken, and messages, in accordance with a code of signals brought out by Kavanagh, were interchanged with the Residency. The 15th was a Sunday; the force did not advance till the afternoon, as it had been decided to wait for the rear-guard and provisions and the spare ammunition, etc., to close up. About two o'clock Peel's guns, covered by the Ninety-Third, advanced, and we drove the enemy from the Martinière and occupied it, the semaphore being then removed from the Dilkusha to the Martinière.

The Ninety-Third held the Martinière and the grounds to the left of it, facing the city, till about two a.m. on Monday the 16th of November, when Captain Peel's battery discharged several rockets as a signal to the Residency that we were about to commence our

march through the city. We were then formed up and served with
some rations, which had been cooked in the rear, each man receiving what was supposed to be three pounds of beef, boiled in salt so
that it would keep, and the usual dozen of commissariat biscuits
and a canteenful of tea cooked on the ground. Just before we started
I saw Sir Colin drinking his tea, the same kind as that served out
to the men, out of a Ninety-Third soldier's canteen.

After getting our three days' rations and tea, the Ninety-Third
were formed up, and the roll was called to see that none, except
those known to be wounded or sick, were missing. Sir Colin again
addressed the men, telling us that there was heavy work before us,
and that we must hold well together, and as much as possible keep
in threes, and that as soon as we stormed a position we were to use
the bayonet. The centre man of each group of three was to make
the attack, and the other two to come to his assistance with their
bayonets right and left. We were not to fire a single bullet after
we got inside a position, unless we were certain of hitting our
enemy, for fear of wounding our own men. To use the bayonet
with effect we were ordered, as I say, to group in threes and
mutually assist each other, for by such action we would soon
bayonet the enemy down although they might be ten to one; which
as a matter of fact they were. It was by strictly following this advice
and keeping cool and mutually assisting each other that the bayonet
was used with such terrible effect inside the Secundrabagh. It was
exactly as Sir Colin had foretold in his address in front of the Alambagh. He knew the sepoys well, that when brought to the point of
the bayonet they could not look the Europeans in the face. For all
that they fought like devils. In addition to their muskets, all the
men in the Secundrabagh were armed with swords from the King
of Oudh's magazines, and the native *tulwars** were as sharp as
razors. When they had fired their muskets, they hurled them
amongst us like javelins, bayonets first, and then drawing their
tulwars, rushed madly on to their destruction, slashing in blind fury
with their swords and using them as one sees sticks used in the
sham fights on the last night of the *Muharram*.† As they rushed
on us shouting '*Din! Din!* (The Faith! the Faith!)' they actually
threw themselves under the bayonets and slashed at our legs. It

* Sabres. [M.E.]
† A Muslim festival in memory of the martyrdom of Hasan and Husain, grandsons of
Muhammad. [M.E.]

was owing to this fact that more than half of our wounded were injured by sword-cuts.

From the Martinière we slowly and silently commenced our advance across the canal, the front of the column being directed by Mr Kavanagh and his native guide. Just as morning broke we had reached the outskirts of a village on the east side of the Secundra-bagh. Here a halt was made for the heavy guns to be brought to the front, three companies of the Ninety-Third with some more artillery being diverted to the left under command of Colonel Leith-Hay, to attack the old Thirty-Second barracks, a large building in the form of a cross strongly flanked with earthworks. The rest of the force advanced through the village by a narrow lane, from which the enemy was driven by us into the Secundrabagh.

About the centre of the village another short halt was made. Here we saw a naked wretch, of a strong muscular build, with his head closely shaven except for the tuft on his crown, and his face all streaked in a hideous manner with white and red paint, his body smeared with ashes. He was sitting on a leopard's skin counting a rosary of beads. A young staff-officer, I think it was Captain A. O. Mayne, Deputy Assistant Quartermaster-General, was making his way to the front, when a man of my company, named James Wilson, pointed to this painted wretch saying, 'I would like to try my bayonet on the hide of that painted scoundrel, who looks a murderer.' Captain Mayne replied: 'Oh don't touch him; these fellows are harmless Hindu *yogis* and won't hurt us. It is the Muhammadans that are to blame for the horrors of this Mutiny.' The words had scarcely been uttered when the painted scoundrel stopped counting the beads, slipped his hand under the leopard skin, and as quick as lightning brought out a short, brass, bell-mouthed blunderbuss and fired the contents of it into Captain Mayne's chest at a distance of only a few feet. His action was as quick as it was unexpected, and Captain Mayne was unable to avoid the shot, or the men to prevent it. Immediately our men were upon the assassin; there was no means of escape for him, and he was quickly bayoneted. Since then I have never seen a painted Hindu, but I involuntarily raise my hand to knock him down. From that hour I formed the opinion that the pampered high-caste Hindu sepoys had far more to do with the Mutiny and the cowardly murders of women and children, than the Muhammadans, although the latter still bear most of the blame.

Immediately after this incident we advanced through the village and came in front of the Secundrabagh, when a murderous fire was opened on us from the loopholed wall and from the windows and flat roof of a two-storied building in the centre of the garden. Having got through the village, our men and the sailors manned the drag-ropes of the heavy guns, and these were run up to within one hundred yards, or even less, of the wall. As soon as the guns opened fire the Infantry Brigade was made to take shelter at the back of a low mud wall behind the guns, the men taking steady aim at every loophole from which we could see the musket-barrels of the enemy protruding. The Commander-in-Chief and his staff were close beside the guns, Sir Colin every now and again turning round when a man was hit, calling out, 'Lie down, Ninety-Third, lie down! Every man of you is worth his weight in gold to England today!'

4. CAPTURE OF THE SECUNDRABAGH

EARLY in the attack on the Secundrabagh three companies of the Ninety-Third were detached under Colonel Leith-Hay to clear the ground to the left and carry the barracks, and Colonel Ewart was left in command of the other seven companies. For some time we lay down sheltered by a low mud wall not more than one hundred and fifty to two hundred yards from the walls of the Secundrabagh, to allow time for the heavy guns to breach the garden wall. During this time Colonel Ewart had dismounted and stood exposed on the bank, picking off the enemy on the top of the building with one of the men's rifles which he took, making the owner of the rifle lie down.

The first shots from our guns passed through the wall, piercing it as though it were a piece of cloth, and without knocking the surrounding brickwork away. Accounts differ, but my impression has always been that it was from half to three-quarters of an hour that the guns battered at the walls. During this time the men, both artillery and sailors,* working the guns without any cover so close to the enemy's loopholes, were falling fast, over two guns' crews having been disabled or killed before the wall was breached. After holes had been pounded through the wall in many places large blocks of brick-and-mortar commenced to fall out, and then portions of the wall came down bodily, leaving wide gaps. Thereupon a sergeant of the Fifty-Third, who had served under Sir Colin Campbell in the Punjab, presuming on old acquaintance, called out: 'Sir Colin, your Excellency, let the infantry storm; let the two "Thirds" at them (meaning the Fifty-Third and Ninety-Third), and we'll soon make short work of the murdering villains!' The sergeant who called to Sir Colin was a Welshman Joe Lee. He was always known as Dobbin in his regiment; and Sir Colin, who had a most wonderful memory for names and faces, turning to General Sir William Mansfield who had formerly served in the Fifty-Third, said, 'Isn't that Sergeant Dobbin?' General Mansfield replied in the affirmative; and Sir Colin, turning to Lee, said, 'Do you think the breach is wide enough, Dobbin?' Lee replied, 'Part

* Belonging to the Naval Brigade. [M.E.]

of us can get through and hold it till the pioneers widen it with their crowbars to allow the rest to get in.' The word was then passed to the Fourth Punjabis to prepare to lead the assault, and after a few more rounds were fired, the charge was ordered. The Punjabis dashed over the mud wall shouting the war-cry of the Sikhs, 'Jai Khalsa Ji!'* led by their two European officers, who were both shot down before they had gone a few yards. This staggered the Sikhs, and they halted. As soon as Sir Colin saw them waver, he turned to Colonel Ewart, who was in command of the seven companies of the Ninety-Third (Colonel Leith-Hay being in command of the assault), and said: 'Colonel Ewart, bring on the tartan—let my own lads at them.' Before the command could be repeated or the buglers had time to sound the advance, the whole seven companies, like one man, leaped over the wall, with such a yell of pent-up rage as I had never heard before nor since. It was not a cheer, but a concentrated yell of rage and ferocity that made the echoes ring again; and it must have struck terror into the defenders, for they actually ceased firing, and we could see them through the breach rushing from the outside wall to take shelter in the two-storied building in the centre of the garden, the gate and doors of which they firmly barred. Here I must not omit to pay a tribute to Pipe-Major John M'Leod, who, with seven pipers, the other three being with their companies attacking the barracks, struck up the Highland Charge, called by some *The Haughs of Cromdell*, and by others *On wi' the Tartan*—the famous charge of the great Montrose when he led his Highlanders so often to victory. When all was over, and Sir Colin complimented the pipe-major on the way he had played, John said, 'I thought the boys would fecht better wi' the national music to cheer them.'

Once inside the Secundrabagh, the Fifty-Third (who got in by a window or small door in the wall to the right of the hole by which we got through) and the Sikhs who followed us, joined the Ninety-Third, and keeping together the bayonet did the work.

It has always been a disputed point who got through the hole first. I believe the first man in was Lance-Corporal Donnelly of the Ninety-Third, who was killed inside; then Subadar Gokul Singh, followed by Sergeant-Major Murray, of the Ninety-Third, also killed, and fourth, Captain Burroughs, severely wounded.

It was about this time I got through myself, pushed up by

* 'Victory to the Sikh people!'

Colonel Ewart who immediately followed. My feet had scarcely touched the ground inside, when a sepoy fired point-blank at me from among the long grass a few yards distant. The bullet struck the thick brass clasp of my waist-belt, but with such force that it sent me spinning heels over head. The man who fired was cut down by Captain Cooper, of the Ninety-Third, who got through the hole abreast with myself. When struck I felt just as one feels when tripped up at a football match. Before I regained my feet, I heard Ewart say as he rushed past me, 'Poor fellow, he is done for.' I was but stunned, and regaining my feet and my breath too, which was completely knocked out of me, I rushed on to the inner court of the building, where I saw Ewart bare-headed, his feather bonnet having been shot off his head, engaged in fierce hand-to-hand fight with several of the enemy. I believe he shot down five or six of them with his revolver. By that time the whole of the Ninety-Third and the Sikhs had got in either through the wall or by the principal gate which had now been forced open; the Fifty-Third, led by Lieutenant-Colonel Gordon of the Ninety-Third, and Captain B. Walton (who was severely wounded), had got in by a window in the right-angle of the garden wall which they forced open. The inner court was rapidly filled with dead, but two officers of the mutineers were fiercely defending a regimental colour inside a dark room. Ewart rushed on them to seize it, and although severely wounded in his sword-arm, he not only captured the colour, but killed both the officers who were defending it.

By this time opposition had almost ceased. A few only of the defenders of the Secundrabagh were left alive, and those few were being hunted out of dark corners, some of them from below heaps of slain. Colonel Ewart, seeing that the fighting was over, started with his colour to present it to Sir Colin Campbell; but whether it was that the old Chief considered that it was *infra dig.* for a field-officer to expose himself to needless danger, or whether it was that he was angry at some other thing, I know not, but this much I remember: Colonel Ewart ran up to him where he sat on his grey charger outside the gate of the Secundrabagh, and called out: 'We are in possession of the bungalows, sir. I have killed the last two of the enemy with my own hand, and here is one of their colours.' 'D—n your colours, sir!' said Sir Colin. 'It's not your place to be taking colours; go back to your regiment this instant, sir!' However, the officers of the staff who were with Sir Colin gave a cheer for Colonel Ewart, and one of them presented him with a cap to cover his head, which was still bare. He turned back, apparently very much upset at the reception given to him by the old Chief; but I afterwards heard that Sir Colin sent for him in the afternoon, apologised for his rudeness, and thanked him for his services. Before I conclude, I may remark that I have often thought over this incident, and the more I think of it, the more I am convinced that, from the wild and excited appearance of Colonel Ewart, who had been by that time more than an hour without his hat in the fierce rays of the sun, covered with blood and powder smoke, and his eyes still flashing with the excitement of the fight, giving him the appearance of a man under the influence of something more potent than 'blue ribbon' tipple—I feel pretty sure, I say, that, when Sir Colin first saw him, he thought he was drunk. When he found out his mistake he was of course sorry for his rudeness.

In the first chapter of these reminiscences I mentioned that, before leaving Dover, the Ninety-Third obtained a number of volunteers from the other Highland regiments serving in England. Ours was the only Highland regiment told off for the China expedition, and it was currently whispered that Lord Elgin had specially asked for us to form his guard of honour at the court of China after he had administered a due castigation to the Chinese. Whether the report was true or not, the belief did the regiment no harm; it added to the *esprit de corps* which was already a prominent feeling in the regiment, and enabled the boys to boast to the girls in Portsmouth that they were 'a cut above' the other corps of the army. In support of this, the fact is worthy of being put on record that although the regiment was not (as is usually the case) confined to barracks the night before embarking, but were allowed leave till midnight, still, when the time to leave the barracks came, there was not a single man absent nor a prisoner in the guard-room; and General Britain put it in garrison orders that he had never been able to say the same of any other corps during the time he had commanded the Portsmouth garrison. But the Ninety-Third were no ordinary regiment. They were then the most Scotch of all the Highland regiments; in brief, they were a military Highland parish, minister and elders complete. The elders were selected from among the men of all ranks—two sergeants, two corporals, and two privates; and I believe it was the only regiment in the army which had a regular service of Communion plate; and in time of peace the Holy Communion, according to the Church of Scotland, was administered by the regimental chaplain twice a year.

Among the volunteers who came from the Seventy-Second was a man named James Wallace. He and six others from the same regiment joined my company. Wallace was not his real name, but he never took anyone into his confidence, nor was he ever known to have any correspondence. He neither wrote nor received any letters, and he was usually so taciturn in his manner that he was known in the company as the Quaker, a name which had followed him from the Seventy-Second. He had evidently received a superior education, for if asked for any information by a more ignorant comrade, he would at once give it; or questioned as to the translation of a Latin or French quotation in a book, he would give it without the least hesitation. I have often seen him on the voyage out walking up and down the deck of the *Belleisle* during the watches of the night, repeating the famous poem of Lamartine, *Le Chien du Solitaire*, commencing:

> Hélas! rentrer tout seul dans sa maison déserte
> Sans voir à votre approche une fenêtre ouverte.

Taking him all in all Quaker Wallace was a strange enigma which no one could solve. When pressed to take promotion, for which his superior education well fitted him, he absolutely refused, always saying that he had come to the Ninety-Third for a certain purpose, and when that purpose was accomplished, he only wished to die.

> With his back to the field, and his feet to the foe!
> And leaving in battle no blot on his name,
> Look proudly to Heaven from the death-bed of fame.

During the march to Lucknow it was a common thing to hear the men in my company say they would give a day's grog to see Quaker Wallace under fire; and the time had now come for their gratification.

There was another man in the company who had joined the regiment in Turkey before embarking for the Crimea. He was also a man of superior education, but in many respects the very antithesis of Wallace. He was both wild and reckless, and used often to receive money sent to him from some one, which he as regularly spent in drink. He went under the name of Hope, but that was also known to be an assumed name, and when the volunteers from the Seventy-Second joined the regiment in Dover, it was remarked that Wallace had the address of Hope, and had asked to be posted to the same company. Yet the two men never spoke to one another; on the contrary they evidently hated each other with a mortal hatred. If the history of these two men could be known it would without doubt form material for a most sensational novel.

Just about the time the men were tightening their belts and preparing for the dash on the breach of the Secundrabagh, this man Hope commenced to curse and swear in such a manner that Captain Dawson, who commanded the company, checked him, telling him that oaths and foul language were no signs of bravery. Hope replied that he did not care a d—— what the captain thought; that he would defy death; that the bullet was not yet moulded that would kill him; and he commenced exposing himself above the mud wall behind which we were lying. The captain was just on the point of ordering a corporal and a file of men to take Hope to the rear-guard as drunk and riotous in presence of the enemy, when Pipe-Major John M'Leod, who was close to the captain, said: 'Don't mind the puir lad, sir; he's not drunk, he is fey! It's not himself that's speaking; he will never see the sun set.' The words were barely out of the pipe-major's mouth when Hope sprang up on the top of the mud wall, and a bullet struck him on the right side, hitting the buckle of his purse belt, which diverted its course, and instead of going right through his body it cut him round the front of his belly below the waist-belt, making a deep wound, and his bowels burst out falling down to his knees. He sank down at once, gasping for breath, when a couple of bullets went through his chest and he died without a groan. John M'Leod turned and said to Captain Dawson, 'I told you so, sir. The lad was fey! I am never deceived in a fey man! It was not himself who spoke when swearing in yon terrible manner.' Just at this time Quaker Wallace, who had evidently been a witness of Hope's tragic end, worked his way along to where the dead man lay, and looking on the distorted features he solemnly said, 'The fool hath said in his heart, there is no God. Vengeance is mine, I will repay, saith the Lord. *I came to the Ninety-Third to see that man die!*' All this happened only a few seconds before the assault was ordered, and attracted but little attention except from those who were immediate witnesses of the incident. The gunners were falling fast, and almost all eyes were turned on them and the breach. When the signal for the assault was given, Quaker Wallace went into the Secundrabagh like one of the Furies, if there are male Furies, plainly seeking death but not meeting it, and quoting the 116th Psalm, Scotch version in metre, beginning at the first verse:

> I love the Lord, because my voice
>> And prayers He did hear.
> I, while I live, will call on Him,
>> Who bow'd to me His ear.

And thus he plunged into the Secundrabagh quoting the next verse at every shot fired from his rifle and at each thrust given by his bayonet:

> I'll of salvation take the cup,
>> On God's name will I call;
> I'll pay my vows now to the Lord
>> Before His people all.

It was generally reported in the company that Quaker Wallace single-handed killed twenty men, and one wonders at this, remembering that he took no comrade with him and did not follow Sir Colin's rule of 'fighting in threes,' but whenever he saw an enemy he went for him! I may here remark that the case of Wallace proved that, in a fight like the Secundrabagh where the enemy is met hand to hand and foot to foot, the way to escape death is to brave it. Of course Wallace might have been shot from a distance, and in that respect he only ran an even chance with the others; but wherever he rushed with his bayonet, the enemy did their utmost to give him a wide berth.

By the time the bayonet had done its work of retribution, the throats of our men were hoarse with shouting 'Cawnpore! you bloody murderers!' The taste of the powder (the muzzle-loading cartridges had to be bitten with the teeth) made men almost mad with thirst; and with the sun high over head, and being fresh from England, with our feather bonnets, red coats, and heavy kilts, we felt the heat intensely.

In the centre of the inner court of the Secundrabagh there was a large *pipal** tree with a very bushy top, round the foot of which were set a number of jars full of cool water. When the slaughter

* Fig tree. [M.E.]

was almost over, many of our men went under the tree for the sake of its shade, and to quench their burning thirst with a draught of the cool water from the jars. A number however lay dead under this tree, both of the Fifty-Third and Ninety-Third, and the many bodies lying in that particular spot attracted the notice of Captain Dawson. After having carefully examined the wounds, he noticed that in every case the men had evidently been shot from above. He thereupon stepped out from beneath the tree, and called to Quaker Wallace to look up if he could see any one in the top of the tree, because all the dead under it had apparently been shot from above. Wallace had his rifle loaded, and stepping back he carefully scanned the top of the tree. He almost immediately called out, 'I see him, sir!' and cocking his rifle he repeated aloud,

> I'll pay my vows now to the Lord
> Before His people all.

He fired, and down fell a body dressed in a tight-fitting red jacket and tight-fitting rose-coloured silk trousers; and the breast of the jacket bursting open with the fall, showed that the wearer was a woman. She was armed with a pair of heavy old-pattern cavalry pistols, one of which was in her belt still loaded, and her pouch was still about half full of ammunition, while from her perch in the tree, which had been carefully prepared before the attack, she had killed more than half-a-dozen men. When Wallace saw that the person whom he shot was a woman, he burst into tears, exclaiming: 'If I had known it was a woman, I would rather have died a thousand deaths than have harmed her.'

By this time all opposition had ceased, and over two thousand of the enemy lay dead within the building and the centre court. The troops were withdrawn, and the muster-roll of the Ninety-Third was called just outside the gate.

When the roll was called it was found that the Ninety-Third had nine officers and ninety-nine men, in all one hundred and eight, killed and wounded. The roll of the Fifty-Third was called alongside of us, and Sir Colin Campbell rode up and addressing the men, spoke out in a clear voice: 'Fifty-Third and Ninety-Third, you have bravely done your share of this morning's work, and Cawnpore is avenged!' Whereupon one of the Fifty-Third sang out, 'Three cheers for the Commander-in-Chief, boys,' which was heartily responded to.

many of the men were wearing the Punjab medals on their breasts.*
This regiment and the Eleventh Oudh Irregulars were simply
annihilated. On examining the bodies of the dead, over fifty men
of the Seventy-First were found to have furloughs, or leave-
certificates, signed by their former commanding officer in their
pockets, showing that they had been on leave when their regiment
mutinied and had rejoined their colours to fight against us.

When the number of the slain was reported to Sir Colin, he
turned to Brigadier Hope, and said: 'This morning's work will
strike terror into the sepoys—it will strike terror into them', and
he repeated it several times. Then turning to us again he said:
'Ninety-Third, you have bravely done your share of this morning's
work, and Cawnpore is avenged! There is more hard work to be
done; but unless as a last resource, I will not call on you to storm
more positions today. Your duty will be to cover the guns after
they are dragged into position. But, my boys, if need be, remember
I depend on you to carry the next position in the same daring
manner in which you carried the Secundrabagh.' With that some
one from the ranks called out, 'Will we get a medal for this, Sir
Colin?' To which he replied: 'Well, my lads, I can't say what Her
Majesty's Government may do; but if you don't get a medal, all I
can say is you have deserved one better than any troops I have ever
seen under fire. I shall inform the Governor-General, and through
him, Her Majesty the Queen, that I have never seen troops behave
better.' The order was then given to man the drag-ropes of Peel's
guns for the advance on the Shah Najaf, and obeyed with a cheer;
and, as it turned out, the Ninety-Third had to storm that position
also.

At the word of command Captain Middleton's battery of Royal
Artillery dashed forward with loud cheers, the drivers waving their
whips and the gunners their caps as they passed us and Peel's guns
at the gallop. The 24-pounder guns meanwhile were dragged along
by our men and the sailors in the teeth of a perfect hail of lead and
iron from the enemy's batteries. In the middle of the march a poor
sailor lad, just in front of me, had his leg carried clean off above the
knee by a round-shot, and, although knocked head over heels by
the force of the shot, he sat bolt upright on the grass, with the
blood spouting from the stump of his limb like water from the hose
of a fire-engine, and shouted, 'Here goes a shilling a day, a shilling

* Gained in the Sikh Wars 1845–6, 1848–9. [M.E.]

a day! Pitch into them, boys, pitch into them! Remember Cawnpore, Ninety-Third, remember Cawnpore! Go at them, my
hearties!' and he fell back in a dead faint, and on we went. I afterwards heard that the poor fellow was dead before a doctor could
reach the spot to bind up his limb.

I will conclude this chapter with an extract from Sir Colin's
despatch on the advance on the Shah Najaf:

The Ninety-Third and Captain Peel's guns rolled on in one
irresistible wave, the men falling fast, but the column advanced till
the heavy guns were within twenty yards of the walls of the Shah
Najaf, where they were unlimbered and poured in round after
round against the massive walls of the building, the withering fire
of the Highlanders covering the Naval Brigade from great loss.
But it was an action almost unexampled in war. Captain Peel
behaved very much as if he had been laying the *Shannon* alongside
an enemy's frigate.

But in this despatch Sir Colin does not mention that he was
himself wounded by a bullet after it had passed through the head
of a Ninety-Third grenadier.

5. FORTUNES AND MISFORTUNES

I MUST now leave for a little the general struggle, and turn to the actions of individual men as they fell under my own observation—actions which neither appear in despatches nor in history. I will now relate a service rendered by Sergeant M. W. Findlay, of my company, which was never noticed nor rewarded. Sergeant Findlay, let me state, merely considered that he had done his duty, but that is no reason why I should not mention his name.

After Captain Peel's guns were dragged into position, the Ninety-Third took up whatever shelter they could get on the right and left of the guns, and I, with several others, got behind the walls of an unroofed mud hut, through which we made loopholes on the side next to the Shah Najaf, and were thus able to keep up a destructive fire on the enemy. Let me add here that the surgeons of the force were overwhelmed with work, and attending to the wounded in the thick of the fire. Some time after the attack had commenced we noticed Captain Alison and his horse in a heap together a few yards behind where we were in shelter. Sergeant Findlay rushed out, got the wounded officer clear of his dead horse under a perfect hail of bullets and round-shot, and carried him under the shelter of the walls where we were lying. He then ran off in search of a surgeon to bandage his wounds, which were bleeding very profusely; but the surgeons were all too busy, and Sir Colin was most strict on the point of wounds being attended to. Officers, no matter what their rank, had no precedence over the rank-and-file in this respect; in fact, Sir Colin often expressed the opinion that an officer could be far more easily replaced than a well-drilled private. However, there was no surgeon available; so Sergeant Findlay took his own bandage—every soldier on going on active service is supplied with lint and a bandage to have them handy in case of wounds—set to work, stanched the bleeding, and bandaged up the wounds of Captain Alison in such a surgeon-like manner that, when Dr Menzies of the Ninety-Third at length came to see him, he thought he had been attended to by a doctor. When he did discover that it was Sergeant Findlay who had put on the bandages, he expressed his surprise, and said that in all probability this prompt action had saved Captain Alison's life, who otherwise might have been weakened by loss of blood beyond recovery before a doctor could have attended to him. Dr Menzies there and then applied to Captain Dawson to get Sergeant Findlay into the field-hospital as an extra assistant to attend to the wounded. In closing this incident I may remark that I have known men get the Victoria Cross for incurring far less danger than Sergeant Findlay did in exposing himself to bring Captain Alison under shelter. The bullets were literally flying round him like hail; several passed through his clothes, and his feather bonnet was shot off his head. When he had finished putting on the bandages he coolly remarked: 'I must go out and get my bonnet for fear I get sunstruck;' so out he went for his hat, and before he got back scores of bullets were fired at him from the walls of the Shah Najaf.

The next man I shall refer to was Sergeant Daniel White, one of the coolest and most fearless men in the regiment. Sergeant White was a man of superior education, an excellent vocalist and reciter, with a most retentive memory, and one of the best amateur actors in the Ninety-Third. Under fire he was just as cool and collected as if he had been enacting the part of Bailie Nicol Jarvie in *Rob Roy*.

In the force defending the Shah Najaf, in addition to the regular army, there was a large body of archers on the walls, armed with bows and arrows which they discharged with great force and precision, and on White raising his head above the wall an arrow was shot right into his feather bonnet. Inside his bonnet, however, he had placed his forage cap, folded up, and instead of passing right through, the arrow stuck in the folds of the forage cap, and 'Dan', as he was called, coolly pulled out the arrow, paraphrasing a quotation from Sir Walter Scott's *Legend of Montrose*, where Dugald Dalgetty and Ranald MacEagh made their escape from the castle of M'Callum More. Looking at the arrow, 'My conscience!' said White, 'bows and arrows! bows and arrows! Have we got Robin Hood and Little John back again? Bows and arrows! My conscience, the sight has not been seen in civilised war for nearly two hundred years. Bows and arrows! And why not weavers' beams as in the days of Goliath? Ah! that Daniel White should be able to tell in the Saut Market of Glasgow that he had seen men fight with bows and arrows in the days of Enfield rifles! Well, well,

Jack Pandy,* since bows and arrows are the words, here's at you!'
and with that he raised his feather bonnet on the point of his
bayonet above the top of the wall, and immediately another arrow
pierced it through, while a dozen more whizzed past a little wide
of the mark.

Just then one poor fellow of the Ninety-Third, named Penny, of
No. 2 company, raising his head for an instant a little above the
wall, got an arrow right through his brain, the shaft projecting
more than a foot out at the back of his head. As the poor lad fell
dead at our feet, Sergeant White remarked, 'Boys, this is no joke;
we must pay them off'. We all loaded and capped, and pushing up
our feather bonnets again, a whole shower of arrows went past or
through them. Up we sprang and returned a well-aimed volley
from our rifles at point-blank distance, and more than half-a-dozen
of the enemy went down. But one unfortunate man of the regiment,
named Montgomery, of No. 6 company, exposed himself a little
too long to watch the effect of our volley, and before he could get
down into shelter again an arrow was sent right through his heart,
passing clean through his body and falling on the ground a few
yards behind him. He leaped about six feet straight up in the air,
and fell stone dead. White could not resist making another quotation, but this time it was from the old English ballad of *Chevy
Chase*.

> He had a bow bent in his hand
>   Made of a trusty tree,
> An arrow of a cloth-yard long
>   Up to the head drew he.
>
> Against Sir Hugh Montgomerie
>   So right his shaft he set,
> The grey goose wing that was thereon
>   In his heart's blood was wet.

Readers who have never been under the excitement of a fight like
this which I describe, may think that such coolness is an exaggeration. It is not so. Remember the men of whom I write had stood in
the 'Thin Red Line' of Balaklava without wavering, and had made
up their minds to die where they stood, if need be; men who had
been for days and nights under shot and shell in the trenches of

* See Introduction, p. 11. [M.E.]

Sebastopol. If familiarity breeds contempt, continual exposure to danger breeds coolness, and, I may say, selfishness too; where all are exposed to equal danger little sympathy is, for the time being at least, displayed for the unlucky ones 'knocked on the head', to use the common expression in the ranks for those who are killed. Besides, Sergeant Daniel White was an exceptionally cool man, and looked on every incident with the eye of an actor.

By this time the sun was getting low, a heavy cloud of smoke hung over the field, and every flash of the guns and rifles could be clearly seen. The enemy in hundreds were visible on the ramparts, yelling like demons, brandishing their swords in one hand and burning torches in the other, shouting at us to 'Come on!' But little impression had been made on the solid masonry walls. Brigadier Hope and his aide-de-camp were rolling on the ground together, the horses of both shot dead; and the same shell which had done this mischief exploded one of our ammunition wagons, killing and wounding several men. Altogether the position looked black and critical when Major Barnston and his battalion of detachments were ordered to storm. This battalion of detachments was a body made up of almost every corps in the service—at least as far as the regiments forming the expedition to China were concerned—and men belonging to the different corps which had entered the Residency with Generals Havelock and Outram. It also comprised some men who had been left (through sickness or wounds) at Allahabad and Cawnpore, and some of the Ninetieth Regiment which had been intercepted at Singapore on their way to China, under Captain Wolseley. However, although a made-up battalion, they advanced bravely to the breach, and I think their leader, Major Barnston, was killed, and the command devolved on Captain Wolseley. He made a most determined attempt to get into the place, but there were no scaling-ladders, and the wall was still almost twenty feet high. During the heavy cannonade the masonry had fallen down in flakes on the outside, but still leaving an inner wall standing almost perpendicular, and in attempting to climb up this the men were raked with a hail of missiles—grenades and round-shot hurled from wall-pieces, arrows and brickbats, burning torches of rags and cotton saturated with oil—even boiling water was dashed on them! In the midst of the smoke the breach would have made a very good representation of Pandemonium. There were scores of men armed with great burning torches just like what one may see in the sham fights of the *Muharram*, only these men were in earnest, shouting *'Allah Akbar!'* *'Din! Din!'* and *'Jai Kali maki!'**

The stormers were driven back, leaving many dead and wounded under the wall. At this juncture Sir Colin called on Brigadier Hope to form up the Ninety-Third for a final attempt. Sir Colin, again addressing us, said that he had not intended to call on us to storm more positions that day, but that the building in our front must be carried before dark, and the Ninety-Third must do it, and he would lead us himself, saying again: 'Remember, men, the lives at stake inside the Residency are those of women and children, and they must be rescued.' A reply burst from the ranks: 'Ay, ay, Sir Colin! we stood by you at Balaklava, and will stand by you here; but you must not expose yourself so much as you are doing. We can be replaced, but you can't. You must remain behind; we can lead ourselves.'

By that time the battalion of detachments had cleared the front, and the enemy were still yelling to us to 'Come on', and piling up missiles to give us a warm reception. Captain Peel had meanwhile brought his infernal machine, known as a rocket battery, to the front, and sent a volley of rockets through the crowd on the ramparts around the breach. Just at that moment Sergeant John Paton of my company came running down the ravine that separated the Kaddam Rasal from the Shah Najaf, completely out of breath through exertion, but just able to tell Brigadier Hope that he had gone up the ravine at the moment the battalion of detachments had been ordered to storm, and had discovered a breach in the northeast corner of the rampart next to the river Gumti. It appears that our shot and shell had gone over the first breach, and had blown out the wall on the other side in this particular spot. Paton told how he had climbed up to the top of the ramparts without difficulty, and seen right inside the place as the whole defending force had been called forward to repulse the assault in front.

Captain Dawson and his company were at once called out, and while the others opened fire on the breach in front of them, we dashed down the ravine, Sergeant Paton showing the way. As soon as the enemy saw that the breach behind had been discovered, and that their well-defended position was no longer tenable, they fled

* 'God is great!' 'The Faith! The Faith!' 'Victory to Mother Kali!' The first two are Muhammadan war-cries; the last is Hindu.

like sheep through the back gate next to the Gumti and another in the direction of the Moti Mahal.* If No. 7 company had got in behind them and cut off their retreat by the back gate, it would have been Secundrabagh over again! As it was, by the time we got over the breach we were able to catch only about a score of the fugitives, who were promptly bayoneted; the rest fled pell-mell into the Gumti, and it was then too dark to see to use the rifle with effect on the flying masses. However, by the great pools of blood inside, and the number of dead floating in the river, they had plainly suffered heavily, and the well-contested position of the Shah Najaf was ours.

By this time Sir Colin and those of his staff remaining alive or unwounded were inside the position, and the front gate thrown open. A hearty cheer was given for the Commander-in-Chief, as he called the officers round him to give instructions for the disposition of the force for the night. As it was Captain Dawson and his company who had scaled the breach, to them was assigned the honour of holding the Shah Najaf, which was now one of the principal positions to protect the retreat from the Residency. And thus ended the terrible 16th of November, 1857.

In the taking of the Secundrabagh all the subaltern officers of my company were wounded, namely, Lieutenants E. Welch and S. E. Wood, and Ensign F. R. M'Namara. The only officer therefore with the company in the Shah Najaf was Captain Dawson. Sergeant Findlay, as already mentioned, had been taken over as hospital-assistant, and another sergeant named Wood was either sick or wounded, I forget which, and Corporals M'Kenzie and Mitchell (a namesake of mine, belonging to Balmoral) were killed. It thus fell to my lot as the non-commissioned officer on duty to go round with Captain Dawson to post the sentries. Mr Kavanagh, who was officiating as a volunteer staff-officer, accompanied us to point out the direction of the strongest positions of the enemy, and the likely points from which any attempts would be made to recapture our position during the night. During the absence of the Captain the command of the company devolved on Colour-Sergeant David Morton, of 'Tobacco Soup' fame, and he was instructed to see that none of the enemy were still lurking in the rooms surrounding the mosque of the Shah Najaf, while the captain was going round the ramparts placing the sentries for the protection of our position.

* The Pearl Mosque.

As soon as the sentries were posted on the ramparts and regular reliefs told off, arrangements were made among the sergeants and corporals to patrol at regular intervals from sentry to sentry to see that all were alert. This was the more necessary as the men were completely worn out and fatigued by long marches and heavy fighting, and in fact had not once had their belts off for a week previous, while all the time carrying double ammunition on half-empty stomachs. Every precaution had therefore to be taken that the sentries should not go to sleep, and it fell to me as the corporal on duty to patrol the first two hours of the night, from eight o'clock till ten. The remainder of the company bivouacked around the piled arms, which were arranged carefully loaded and capped with bayonets fixed, ready for instant action should an attack be made on our position. After the great heat of the day the night by contrast felt bitterly cold. There was a stack of dry wood in the centre of the grounds from which the men kindled a large fire near the piled arms, and arranged themselves around it, rolled in their greatcoats but fully accoutred, ready to stand to arms at the least alarm.

An adventure happened to me in the Shah Najaf which gave me such a nervous fright that I often dream of it. I have forgotten to state that when the force advanced from the Alambagh each man carried his greatcoat rolled into what was then known in our regiment as the 'Crimean roll', with ends strapped together across the right shoulder just over the ammunition pouch-belt, so that it did not interfere with the free use of the rifle, but rather formed a protection across the chest. As it turned out many men owed their lives to the fact that bullets became spent in passing through the rolled greatcoats before reaching a vital part. Now it happened that in the heat of the fight in the Secundrabagh my greatcoat was cut right through where the two ends were fastened together, by the stroke of a keen-edged *tulwar* which was intended to cut me across the shoulder, and as it was very warm at the time from the heat of the midday sun combined with the excitement of the fight, I was rather glad than otherwise to be rid of the greatcoat; and when the fight was over, it did not occur to me to appropriate another one in its place from one of my dead comrades. But by ten o'clock at night there was a considerable difference in the temperature from ten in the morning, and when it came to my turn to be relieved from patrol duty and to lie down for a sleep, I felt the cold wet grass anything but comfortable, and missed my greatcoat to wrap round my knees; for the kilt is not the most suitable dress imaginable for a bivouac, without greatcoat or plaid, on a cold, dewy November night in Upper India; with a raw north wind the climate of Lucknow feels uncommonly cold at night in November, especially when contrasted with the heat of the day.

I have already mentioned that the sun had set before we entered the Shah Najaf, the surrounding enclosure of which contained a number of small rooms round the inside of the walls, arranged after the manner of the ordinary Indian native travellers' *serais*. The Shah Najaf, it must be remembered, was the tomb of Ghazi-ud-din, the first king of Oudh, and consequently a place of Muhammadan pilgrimage, and the small rooms round the four walls of the square were for the accommodation of pilgrims. These rooms had been turned into quarters by the enemy, and, in their hurry to escape, many of them had left their lamps burning, consisting of the ordinary *chirags** placed in small niches in the walls, leaving also their evening meal of *chupatties* in small piles ready cooked, and the curry and *dhal†* boiling on the fires. Many of the lamps were still burning when my turn of duty was over, and as I felt the want of a greatcoat badly, I asked the colour-sergeant of the company (the captain being fast asleep) for permission to go out of the gate to where our dead were collected near the Secundrabagh to get another one. This Colour-Sergeant Morton refused, stating that before going to sleep the captain had given strict orders that except those on sentry no man was to leave his post on any pretence whatever. I had therefore to try to make the best of my position, but although dead tired and wearied out I felt too uncomfortable to go to sleep, and getting up it struck me that some of the sepoys in their hurried departure might have left their greatcoats or blankets behind them. With this hope I went into one of the rooms where a lamp was burning, took it off its shelf, and shading the flame with my hand walked to the door of the great domed tomb, or mosque, which was only about twenty or thirty yards from where the arms were piled and the men lying round the still burning fire.

I peered into the dark vault, not knowing that it was a king's tomb, but could see nothing, so I advanced slowly, holding the

* Little clay saucers of oil, with a loosely twisted cotton wick.
† Small pulse.

chirag high over my head and looking cautiously around for fear of surprise from a concealed enemy, till I was near the centre of the great vault, where my progress was obstructed by a big black heap about four or five feet high, which felt to my feet as if I were walking among loose sand. I lowered the lamp to see what it was, and immediately discovered that I was standing up to the ankles in *loose gunpowder!* About forty cwt. of it lay in a great heap in front of my nose, while a glance to my left showed me a range of twenty to thirty barrels also full of powder, and on the right over a hundred 8-inch shells, all loaded with the fuses fixed, while spare fuses and slow matches and port-fires in profusion lay heaped beside the shells.

By this time my eyes had become accustomed to the darkness of the mosque, and I took in my position and my danger at a glance. Here I was up to my knees in powder—in the very bowels of a magazine with a naked light! My hair literally stood on end; I felt the skin of my head lifting my feather bonnet off my scalp; my knees knocked together, and despite the chilly night air the cold perspiration burst out all over me and ran down my face and legs. I had neither cloth nor handkerchief in my pocket, and there was not a moment to be lost, as already the overhanging wick of the *chirag* was threatening to shed its smouldering red tip into the live magazine at my feet with consequences too frightful to contemplate. Quick as thought I put my left hand under the down-dropping flame, and clasped it with a grasp of determination; holding it firmly I slowly turned to the door, and walked out with my knees knocking one against the other! Fear had so overcome all other feeling that I am confident I never felt the least pain from grasping the burning wick till after I was outside the building and once again in the open air; but when I opened my hand I felt the smart acutely enough. I poured the oil out of the lamp into the burnt hand, and kneeling down thanked God for having saved myself and all the men lying around me from horrible destruction. I then got up and staggering rather than walking to the place where Captain Dawson was sleeping, and shaking him by the shoulder till he awoke, I told him of my discovery and the fright I had got.

At first he either did not believe me, or did not comprehend the danger. 'Bah! Corporal Mitchell,' was all his answer, 'you have woke up out of your sleep, and have got frightened at a shadow,' for my heart was still thumping against my ribs worse than it was when I first discovered my danger, and my voice was trembling. I turned my smarting hand to the light of the fire and showed the captain how it was scorched; and then, feeling my pride hurt at being told I had got frightened at a shadow, I said: 'Sir, you're not a Highlander or you would know the Gaelic proverb *"The heart of one who can look death in the face will not start at a shadow,"* and you, sir, can yourself bear witness that I have not shirked to look death in the face more than once since daylight this morning.' He replied, 'Pardon me, I did not mean that; but calm yourself and explain what it is that has frightened you.' I then told him that I had gone into the mosque with a naked lamp burning, and had found it half full of loose gunpowder piled in a great heap on the floor and a large number of loaded shells. 'Are you sure you're not dreaming from the excitement of this terrible day?' said the captain. With that I looked down to my feet and my gaiters, which were still covered with blood from the slaughter in the Secundra-bagh; the wet grass had softened it again, and on this the powder was sticking nearly an inch thick. I scraped some of it off, throwing it into the fire, and said, 'There is positive proof for you that I'm not dreaming, nor my vision a shadow!' On that the captain became almost as alarmed as I was, and a sentry was posted near the door of the mosque to prevent anyone from entering it. The sleeping men were aroused, and the fire smothered out with as great care as possible, using for the purpose several earthen *ghurrahs*, or jars of water, which the enemy had left under the trees near where we were lying.

When all was over, Colour-Sergeant Morton coolly proposed to the captain to place me under arrest for having left the pile of arms after he, the colour-sergeant, had refused to give me leave. To this proposal Captain Dawson replied: 'If any one deserves to be put under arrest it is you yourself, Sergeant Morton, for not having explored the mosque and discovered the gunpowder while Corporal Mitchell and I were posting the sentries; and if this neglect comes to the notice of either Colonel Hay or the Commander-in-Chief, both you and I are likely to hear more about it; so the less you say about the matter the better!' This ended the discussion and my adventure, and at the time I was glad to hear nothing more about it, but I have sometimes since thought that if the part I acted in this crisis had come to the knowledge of either Colonel Hay or Sir Colin Campbell, my burnt hand would have brought me something more than a proposal to place me under arrest, and take my corporal's stripes from me! Be that as it may, I got a fright that I have never forgotten.

After a sentry had been posted on the mosque and the fire put out, a glass lantern was discovered in one of the rooms, and Captain Dawson and I, with an escort of three or four men, made the circuit of the walls, searching every room. I remember one of the escort was James Wilson, the same man who wished to bayonet the Hindu *yogi* in the village who afterwards shot poor Captain Mayne as told in an earlier chapter. As Wilson was peering into one of the rooms, a concealed sepoy struck him over the head with his *tulwar*, but the feather bonnet saved his scalp as it had saved many more that day, and Captain Dawson being armed with a pair of double-barrelled pistols, put a bullet through the sepoy before he had time to make another cut at Wilson. In the same room I found a good cotton quilt which I promptly annexed to replace my lost greatcoat.

After all was quiet, the men rolled off to sleep again, and wrapping round my legs my newly-acquired quilt, which was lined with silk and had evidently belonged to a rebel officer, I too lay down and tried to sleep. My nerves were however too much shaken, and the pain of my burnt hand kept me awake, so I lay and listened to the men sleeping around me; and what a night that was! Had I the descriptive powers of a Tennyson or a Scott I might draw a picture of it, but as it is I can only very faintly attempt to make my readers imagine what it was like. The horrible scenes through which the men had passed during the day had told with terrible effect on their nervous systems, and the struggles—eye to eye, foot to foot, and steel to steel—with death in the Secundrabagh, were fought over again by most of the men in their sleep, oaths and shouts of defiance often curiously intermingled with prayers. One man would be lying calmly sleeping and commence muttering something inaudible, and then break out into a fierce battle-cry of 'Cawnpore, you bloody murderer!'; another would shout 'Charge! give them the bayonet!'; and a third, 'Keep together, boys, don't fire, forward, forward; if we are to die, let us die like men!' Then I would hear one muttering, 'Oh, mother, forgive me, and I'll never leave you again!'; while his comrade would half rise up, wave his hand, and call, 'There they are! Fire low, give them the bayonet! Remember Cawnpore!' And so it was throughout that memorable night inside the Shah Najaf; and I have no doubt but it was the same with the men holding the other posts. The pain of my burnt hand and the terrible fright I had got kept me awake, and I lay and listened till nearly daybreak; but at length completely worn out, I, too, dosed off into a disturbed slumber, and I suppose I must have behaved in much the same way as those I had been listening to, for I dreamed of blood and battle, and then my mind would wander to scenes on Dee and Don side, and to the Braemar and Lonach gathering, and from that the scene would suddenly change, and I was a little boy again, kneeling beside my mother, saying my evening hymn. Verily that night convinced me that Campbell's *Soldier's Dream* is no mere fiction, but must have been written or dictated from actual experience by one who had passed through such another day of excitement and danger as that of the 16th of November, 1857.

My dreams were rudely broken into by the crash of a round-shot through the top of the tree under which I was lying, and I jumped up repeating aloud the seventh verse of the ninety-first Psalm, Scotch version:

> A thousand at thy side shall fall,
> On thy right hand shall lie
> Ten thousand dead; yet unto thee
> It shall not once come nigh.

Captain Dawson and the sergeants of the company had been astir long before, and a party of ordnance-lascars from the ammunition park and several warrant-officers of the Ordnance-Department were busy removing the gunpowder from the tomb of the Shah Najaf. Over sixty *maunds** of loose powder were filled into bags and carted out, besides twenty barrels of the ordinary size of powder-barrels, and more than one hundred and fifty loaded 8-inch shells. The work of removal was scarcely completed before the enemy commenced firing shell and red-hot round-shot from their batteries in the Padshahbagh across the Gumti, aimed straight for the door of the tomb facing the river, showing that they believed the powder was still there, and that they hoped they might manage to blow us all up.

Immediately after the powder left by the enemy had been removed from the tomb of the Shah Najaf, and the sun had dispelled

* Nearly five thousand lb.

the fog which rested over the Gumti and the city, it was deemed
necessary to signal to the Residency to let them know our position,
and for this purpose our adjutant, Lieutenant William M'Bean,
Sergeant Hutchinson, and Drummer Ross, a boy of about twelve
years of age but even small for his years, climbed to the top of the
dome of the Shah Najaf by means of a rude rope-ladder which was
fixed on it; thence with the regimental colour of the Ninety-Third
and a feather bonnet on the tip of the staff they signalled to the
Residency, and the little drummer sounded the regimental call on
his bugle from the top of the dome. The signal was seen, and
answered from the Residency by lowering their flag three times.
But the enemy in the Padshahbagh also saw the signalling and the
daring adventurers on the dome, and turned their guns on them,
sending several round-shots quite close to them. Their object
being gained, however, our men descended; but little Ross ran up
the ladder again like a monkey, and holding on to the spire of the
dome with his left hand he waved his feather bonnet and then
sounded the regimental call a second time, which he followed by
the call known as *The Cock of the North*, which he sounded as a blast
of defiance to the enemy. When peremptorily ordered to come
down by Lieutenant M'Bean, he did so, but not before the little
monkey had tootled out—

> There's not a man beneath the moon,
>   Nor lives in any land he,
> That hasn't heard the pleasant tune
>   Of Yankee Doodle Dandy!
>
> In cooling drinks and clipper ships,
>   The Yankee has the way shown,
> On land and sea 'tis he that whips
>   Old Bull, and all creation.

When little Ross reached the parapet at the foot of the dome,
he turned to Lieutenant M'Bean and said: 'Ye ken, sir, I was born
when the regiment was in Canada when my mother was on a visit
to an aunt in the States, and I could not come down till I had sung
Yankee Doodle, to make my American cousins envious when they
hear of the deeds of the Ninety-Third. Won't the Yankees feel
jealous when they hear that the littlest drummer-boy in the regiment sang *Yankee Doodle* under a hail of fire on the dome of the
highest mosque in Lucknow!'

Outlying pickets of the Highland Brigade

6. RELIEF OF THE RESIDENCY

BY this time several of the old campaigners had kindled a fire in one of the small rooms, through the roof of which one of our shells had fallen the day before, making a convenient chimney for the egress of the smoke. They had found a large copper pot which had been left by the sepoys, and had it on the fire filled with a stew of about a score or more of pigeons which had been left shut up in a dovecot in a corner of the compound. There were also plenty of pumpkins and other vegetables in the rooms, and piles of *chupatties* which had been cooked by the sepoys for their evening meal before they fled. Everything in fact was there for making a good breakfast for hungry men except salt, and there was no salt to be found in any of the rooms; but as luck favoured us, I had one of the old-fashioned round cylinder-shaped wooden match-boxes full of salt in my haversack, which was more than sufficient to season the stew. I had carried this salt from Cawnpore, and I did so by the advice of an old veteran who had served in the Ninety-Second Gordon Highlanders all through the Peninsular war, and finally at Waterloo. When as a boy I had often listened to his stories and told him that I would also enlist for a soldier, he had given me this piece of practical advice, which I in my turn present to every young soldier and volunteer. It is this: 'Always carry a box of salt in your haversack when on active service; because the commissariat department is usually in the rear, and as a rule when an army is pressed for food the men have often the chance of getting hold of a bullock or a sheep, or of fowls, etc., but it is more difficult to find salt, and even good food without salt is very unpalatable.' I remembered the advice, and it proved of great service to myself and comrades in many instances during the Mutiny. As it was, thanks to my foresight the hungry men in the Shah Najaf made a good breakfast on the morning of the 17th of November, 1857. I may here say that my experience is that the soldiers who could best look after their stomachs were also those who could make the best use of the bayonet, and who were the least likely to fall behind in a forced march. If I had the command of an army in the field my rule would be: 'Cut the grog, and give double grub when hard work has to be done!'

After making a good breakfast the men were told off in sections, and we discharged our rifles at the enemy across the Gumti, and then sponged them out, which they sorely needed, because they had not been cleaned from the day we advanced from the Alambagh. Our rifles had in fact got so foul with four days' heavy work that it was almost impossible to load them, and the recoil had become so great that the shoulders of many of the men were perfectly black with bruises. As soon as our rifles were cleaned, a number of the best shots in the company were selected to try and silence the fire from the battery in the Padshahbagh across the river, which was annoying us by endeavouring to pitch hot shot and shell into the tomb, and to shorten the distance they had brought their guns outside the gate on to the open ground. They evidently as yet did not understand the range of the Enfield rifle, as they now came within about a thousand to twelve hundred yards of the wall of the Shah Najaf next the river. Some twenty of the best shots in the company, with carefully cleaned and loaded rifles, watched till they saw a good number of the enemy near their guns, then, raising sights to the full height and carefully aiming high, they fired a volley by word of command slowly given—*one, two, fire!* and about half a dozen of the enemy were knocked over. They at once withdrew their guns inside the Padshahbagh and shut the gate, and did not molest us any more.

During the early part of the forenoon we had several men struck by rifle bullets fired from one of the minarets in the Moti Mahal, which was said to be occupied by one of the ex-King of Oudh's eunuchs who was a first-rate marksman, and armed with an excellent rifle; from his elevated position in the minaret he could see right into the square of the Shah Najaf. We soon had several men wounded, and as there was no surgeon with us Captain Dawson sent me back to where the field-hospital was formed near the Secundrabagh, to ask Dr Munro if an assistant-surgeon could be spared for our post. But Dr Munro told me to tell Captain Dawson that it was impossible to spare an assistant-surgeon or even an apothecary, because he had just been informed that the Mess-House and Moti Mahal were to be assaulted at two o'clock, and every medical officer would be required on the spot; but he would try and send a hospital-attendant with a supply of lint and bandages. By the time I got back the assault on the Mess-House had begun, and Sergeant Findlay, before mentioned, was sent with a *dooly* and a supply of bandages, lint, and dressing, to do the best he could for any of ours who might be wounded.

About half an hour after the assault on the Mess-House had commenced a large body of the enemy, numbering at least six or seven hundred men, whose retreat had evidently been cut off from the city, crossed from the Mess-House into the Moti Mahal in our front, and forming up under cover of some huts between the Shah Munzil and Moti Mahal, they evidently made up their minds to try and retake the Shah Najaf. They debouched on the plain with a number of men in front carrying scaling-ladders, and Captain Dawson being on the alert ordered all the men to kneel down behind the loopholes with rifles sighted for five hundred yards, and wait for the word of command. It was now our turn to know what it felt like to be behind loopholed walls, and we calmly awaited the enemy, watching them forming up for a dash on our position. The silence was profound, when Sergeant Daniel White repeated aloud a passage from the third canto of Scott's *Bridal of Triermain*:

> Bewcastle now must keep the Hold,
>> Speir-Adam's steeds must bide in stall,
> Of Hartley-burn the bowmen bold
>> Must only shoot from battled wall;
> And Liddesdale may buckle spur,
>> And Teviot now may belt the brand,
> Taras and Ewes keep nightly stir,
>> And Eskdale foray Cumberland.
> Of wasted fields and plunder'd flocks
>> The Borderers bootless may complain;
> They lack the sword of brave De Vaux,
>> There comes no aid from Triermain.

Captain Dawson, who had been steadily watching the advance of the enemy and carefully calculating their distance, just then called 'Attention, five hundred yards, ready—*one, two, fire!*' when over eighty rifles rang out, and almost as many of the enemy went down like ninepins on the plain! Their leader was in front, mounted on a finely-accoutred charger, and he and his horse were evidently both hit; he at once wheeled round and made for the Gumti, but horse and man both fell before they got near the river. After the first volley every man loaded and fired independently, and the plain was soon strewn with dead and wounded.

The unfortunate assaulters were now between two fires, for the
force that had attacked the Shah Munzil and Moti Mahal commenced to send grape and canister into their rear, so the routed
rebels threw away their arms and scaling-ladders, and all that were
able to do so bolted pell-mell for the Gumti. Only about a quarter
of the original number, however, reached the opposite bank, for
when they were in the river our men rushed to the corner nearest
to them and kept peppering at every head above water. One tall
fellow, I well remember, acted as cunningly as a jackal; whether
struck or not he fell just as he got into shallow water on the
opposite side, and lay without moving, with his legs in the water
and his head on the land. He appeared to be stone dead, and every
rifle was turned on those that were running across the plain for the
gate of the Padshahbagh, while many others who were evidently
severely wounded were fired on as our fellows said, *'in mercy to
put them out of pain.'* I have previously remarked that the war of the
Mutiny was a horrible, I may say a demoralising, war for civilised
men to be engaged in. The inhuman murders and foul treachery of
the Nana Sahib and others put all feeling of humanity or mercy for
the enemy out of the question, and our men thus early spoke of
putting a wounded Jack Pandy *out of pain*, just as calmly as if he
had been a wild beast; it was even considered an act of mercy. It is
now horrible to recall it all, but what I state is true. The only
excuse is that *we* did not begin this war of extermination; and no
apologist for the mutineers can say that they were actuated by
patriotism to throw off the yoke of the oppressor. The cold-
blooded cruelty of the mutineers and their leaders from first to last
branded them in fact as traitors to humanity and cowardly assassins
of helpless women and children. But to return to the Pandy whom
I left lying half-covered with water on the further bank of the
Gumti opposite the Shah Najaf. This particular man was ever after
spoken of as the 'jackal', because jackals and foxes have often been
known to sham dead and wait for a chance of escape; and so it was
with Jack Pandy. After he had lain apparently dead for about an
hour, some one noticed that he had gradually dragged himself out
of the water; till all at once he sprang to his feet, and ran like a
deer in the direction of the gate of the Padshahbagh. He was still
quite within easy range, and several rifles were levelled at him;
but Sergeant Findlay, who was on the rampart, and was himself
one of the best shots in the company, called out, 'Don't fire, men;

give the poor devil a chance!' Instead of a volley of bullets, the men's better feelings gained the day, and Jack Pandy was reprieved, with a cheer to speed him on his way. As soon as he heard it he realised his position, and like the Samaritan leper of old, he halted, turned round, and putting up both his hands with the palms together in front of his face, he salaamed profoundly, prostrating himself three times on the ground by way of thanks, and then *walked* slowly towards the Padshahbagh while we on the ramparts waved our feather bonnets and clapped our hands to him in token of good-will. I have often wondered if that particular Pandy ever after fought the English, or if he returned to his village to relate his exceptional experience of our clemency.

Just at this time we noticed a great commotion in front, and heard our fellows and even those in the Residency cheering like mad. The cause we shortly after learned; that the generals, Sir Colin Campbell, Havelock, and Outram had met. The Residency was relieved and the women and children were saved, although not yet out of danger, and every man in the force slept with a lighter heart that night. If the cost was heavy, the gain was great.

Such was the glorious issue of the 17th of November. The meeting of the Generals, Sir Colin Campbell, Outram, and Havelock, proved that Lucknow was relieved and the women and children were safe; but to accomplish this object our small force had lost no less than forty-five officers and four hundred and ninety-six men—more than a tenth of our whole number! The brunt of the loss fell on the Artillery and Naval Brigade, and on the Fifty-Third, the Ninety-Third, and the Fourth Punjab Infantry. These losses were respectively as follows:

Artillery and Naval Brigade	105	men
Fifty-Third Regiment	76	,,
Ninety-Third Highlanders	108	,,
Fourth Punjab Infantry	95	,,
Total	384	

leaving one hundred and twelve to be divided among the other corps engaged.

The Residency was relieved on the afternoon of the 17th of

November, and the following day preparations were made for the evacuation of the position and the withdrawal of the women and children. To do this in safety however was no easy task, for the mutineers and rebels showed but small regard for the laws of chivalry; a man might pass an exposed position in comparative safety, but if a helpless woman or little child were seen, they were made the target for a hundred bullets. So far as we could see from the Shah Najaf, the line of retreat was pretty well sheltered till the refugees emerged from the Moti Mahal; but between that and the Shah Najaf there was a long stretch of plain, exposed to the fire of the enemy's artillery and sharp-shooters from the opposite side of the Gumti. To protect this part of the route a covered trench was constructed: a battery of artillery and some of Peel's guns, with a covering force of infantry, were posted in the north-east corner of the Moti Mahal; and all the best shots in the Shah Najaf were placed on the north-west corner of the ramparts next to the Gumti. These men were under command of Sergeant Findlay, who, although nominally our medical officer, stuck to his post on the ramparts, and being one of the best shots in the company was entrusted with the command of the sharp-shooters for the protection of the retreating women and children. From these two points —the north-east corner of the Moti Mahal and the north-west of the Shah Najaf—the enemy on the north bank of the Gumti were brought under a cross-fire, the accuracy of which made them keep a very respectful distance from the river, with the result that the women and children passed the exposed part of their route without a single casualty. I remember one remarkably good shot made by Sergeant Findlay. He unhorsed a rebel officer close to the east gate of the Padshahbagh, who came out with a force of infantry and a couple of guns to open fire on the line of retreat; but he was no sooner knocked over than the enemy retreated into the bagh, and did not show themselves any more that day.

By midnight of the 22nd of November the Residency was entirely evacuated, and the enemy completely deceived as to the movements; and about two o'clock on the morning of the 23rd we withdrew from the Shah Najaf and became the rear-guard of the retreating column, making our way slowly past the Secundrabagh, the stench from which, as can easily be imagined, was something frightful. I have seen it stated that the two thousand odd of the enemy killed in the Secundrabagh were dragged out and buried in deep trenches outside the enclosure. This is not correct. The European slain were removed and buried in a deep trench, to the east of the gate, and the Punjabis recovered their slain and cremated them near the bank of the Gumti. But the rebel dead had to be left to rot where they lay, a prey to the vulture by day and the jackal by night, for from the smallness of the relieving force no other course was possible; in fact, it was with the greatest difficulty that men could be spared from the piquets—for the whole force simply became a series of outlying piquets—to bury our own dead, let alone those of the enemy. And when we retired their friends did not take the trouble, as the skeletons were still whitening in the rooms of the buildings when the Ninety-Third returned to the siege of Lucknow in March, 1858.

By daylight on the 23rd of November the whole of the women and children had arrived at the Dilkusha, where tents were pitched for them, and the rear-guard had reached the Martinière. Here the rolls were called again to see if any were missing, when it was discovered that Sergeant Alexander Macpherson, of No. 2 company, who had formed one of Colonel Ewart's detachment in the barracks, was not present. Shortly afterwards he was seen making his way across the plain, and reported that he had been left asleep in the barracks, and, on waking up after daylight and finding himself alone, guessed what had happened, and knowing the direction in which the column was to retire, he at once followed. Fortunately the enemy had not even then discovered the evacuation of the Residency, for they were still firing into our old positions. Sergeant Macpherson was ever after this known in the regiment as 'Sleepy Sandy'.

There was also an officer, Captain Waterman, left asleep in the Residency. He, too, managed to join the rear-guard in safety; but he got such a fright that I afterwards saw it stated in one of the Calcutta papers that his mind was affected by the shock to his nervous system. An Irishman in the Ninety-Third gave a good reason why the fright did not turn the head of Sandy Macpherson. Some time— about a month or six weeks—after the events above related, when the Calcutta papers got back to camp with the accounts of the relief of Lucknow, I and Sergeant Macpherson were on outlying piquet at Fatehgarh (I think), and the captain of the piquet gave me a bundle of the newspapers to read out to the men. In these papers there was an account of Captain Waterman's being left behind in the Residency, in which it was stated that the shock had affected his intellect. When I read this out, the men made some remarks concerning the fright which it must have given Sandy Macpherson when he found himself alone in the barracks, and Sandy joining in the remarks, was inclined to boast that the fright had not upset *his* intellect, when an Irishman of the piquet, named Andrew M'Onvill, usually called 'Handy·Andy' in the company, joining in the conversation, said: 'Boys, if Sergeant Macpherson will give me permission, I will tell you a story that will show the reason why the fright did not upset his intellect.' Permission was of course granted for the story, and Handy Andy proceeded with his illustration as follows, as nearly as I can remember it.

'You have all heard of Mr Gough, the great American Temperance lecturer. Well, the year before I enlisted he came to Armagh, giving a course of temperance lectures, and all the public-house keepers and brewers were up in arms to raise as much opposition as possible against Mr Gough and his principles, and in one of his lectures he laid great stress on the fact that he considered moderation the parent of drunkenness. A brewer's drayman thereupon went on the platform to disprove this assertion by actual facts from his own experience, and in his argument in favour of *moderate* drinking, he stated that for upwards of twenty years he had habitually consumed over a gallon of beer and about a pint of whisky daily, and solemnly asserted that he had never been the worse for liquor in his life. To which Mr Gough replied: "My friends, there is no rule without its exception, and our friend here is an exception to the general rule of moderate drinking; but I will tell you a story that I think exactly illustrates his case. Some years ago, when I was a boy, my father had two negro servants, named Uncle Sambo and Snowball. Near our house there was a branch of one of the large fresh-water lakes which swarmed with fish, and it was the duty of Snowball to go every morning to catch sufficient for the breakfast of the household. The way Snowball usually caught his fish was by making them drunk by feeding them with Indian corn-meal mixed with strong whisky and rolled into balls. When these whisky balls were thrown into the water the fish came and ate them readily, but after they had swallowed a few they became helplessly drunk, turning on their backs and allowing themselves to be caught, so that in a very short time Snowball would return with his basket full of fish. But as I said, there is no rule without an exception, and one morning proved that there is also an exception in the matter of fish becoming drunk. As usual Snowball went to the lake with an allowance of whisky balls, and spying a fine big fish with a large flat head, he dropped a ball in front of it, which it at once ate and then another, and another, and so on till all the whisky balls in Snowball's basket were in the stomach of this queer fish, and still it showed no signs of becoming drunk, but kept wagging its tail and looking for more whisky balls. On this Snowball returned home and called old Uncle Sambo to come and see this wonderful fish which had swallowed nearly a peck of whisky balls and still was not drunk. When old Uncle Sambo set eyes on the fish, he exclaimed, 'O Snowball, Snowball! you foolish boy, you will never be able to make that fish drunk with your whisky balls. That fish could live in a barrel of whisky and not get drunk. That fish, my son, is called a mullet-head: it has got no brains.' And that accounts," said Mr Gough, turning to the brewer's drayman, "for our friend here being able for twenty years to drink a gallon of beer and a pint of whisky daily and never become drunk." And so, my chums,' said Handy Andy, 'if you will apply the same reasoning to the cases of Sergeant Macpherson and Captain Waterman I think you will come to the correct conclusion why the fright did not upset the intellect of Sergeant Macpherson.' We all joined in the laugh at Handy Andy's story, and none more heartily than the butt of it, Sandy Macpherson himself.

But enough of digression. Shortly after the roll was called at the Martinière, a most unfortunate accident took place. Corporal Cooper and four or five men went into one of the rooms of the Martinière in which there was a quantity of loose powder which had been left by the enemy, and somehow—it was never known how—the powder got ignited and they were all blown up, their bodies completely charred and their eyes scorched out. The poor fellows all died in the greatest agony within an hour or so of the accident, and none of them ever spoke to say how it happened. The quantity of powder was not sufficient to shatter the house, but it blew the doors and windows out, and burnt the poor fellows as black as charcoal. This sad accident cast a gloom over the regiment, and made me again very mindful of and thankful for my own narrow escape, and that of my comrades in the Shah Najaf on that memorable night of the 16th of November.

Later in the day our sadness increased when it was found that

Colour-Sergeant Alexander Knox, of No. 2 company, was missing. He had called the roll of his company at daylight, and had then gone to see a friend in the Seventy-Eighth Highlanders. He had stayed some time with his friend and left to return to his own regiment, but was never heard of again. Poor Knox had two brothers in the regiment, and he was the youngest of the three. He was a most deserving and, popular non-commissioned officer, decorated with the French war medal and the Cross of the Legion of Honour for valour in the Crimea, and was about to be promoted sergeant-major of the regiment, *vice* Murray killed in the Secundrabagh. His fate was never known.

About two o'clock in the afternoon, the regiment being all together again, the following general order was read to us.

HEADQUARTERS, LA MARTINIERE, LUCKNOW
23rd November, 1857

1. The Commander-in-Chief has reason to be thankful to the force he conducted for the relief of the garrison of Lucknow.

2. Hastily assembled, fatigued by forced marches, but animated by a common feeling of determination to accomplish the duty before them, all ranks of this force have compensated for their small number, in the execution of a most difficult duty, by unceasing exertions.

3. From the morning of the 16th till last night the whole force has been one outlying piquet, never out of fire, and covering an immense extent of ground, to permit the garrison to retire scatheless and in safety covered by the whole of the relieving force.

4. That ground was won by fighting as hard as it ever fell to the lot of the Commander-in-Chief to witness, it being necessary to bring up the same men over and over again to fresh attacks; and it is with the greatest gratification that his Excellency declares he never saw men behave better.

5. The storming of the Secundrabagh and the Shah Najaf has never been surpassed in daring, and the success of it was most brilliant and complete.

6. The movement of retreat of last night, by which the final rescue of the garrison was effected, was a model of discipline and exactness. The consequence was that the enemy was completely deceived, and the force retired by a narrow, tortuous lane, the only line of retreat open, in the face of 50,000 enemies, without molestation.

7. The Commander-in-Chief offers his sincere thanks to Major-General Sir James Outram, G.C.B., for the happy manner in which he planned and carried out his arrangements for the evacuation of the Residency of Lucknow.

By order of his Excellency the Commander-in-Chief,

w. mayhew, *Major*
Deputy Adjutant-General of the Army

Thus were achieved the relief and evacuation of the Residency of Lucknow.* The enemy did not discover that the Residency was deserted till noon on the 23rd, and about the time the above general order was being read to us they fired a salute of one hundred and one guns, but did not attempt to follow us or to cut off our retreat. That night we bivouacked in the Dilkusha park, and retired on the Alambagh on the 25th, the day on which the brave and gallant Havelock died.†

---

* It must always be recollected that this was the *second* relief of Lucknow. The first was effected by the force under Havelock and Outram on the 25th September, 1857, and was in fact more of a reinforcement than a relief.

† Havelock actually died on the evening of the 24th, of dysentery. The troops retired on the Alambagh the next day. [M.E.]

7. RETURN TO CAWNPORE

WE rested at the Alambagh on the 26th of November, but early on the 27th we understood something had gone wrong in our rear, because, as usual with Sir Colin when he contemplated a forced march, we were served out with three days' rations and double ammunition—sixty rounds in our pouches and sixty in our haversacks; and by two o'clock in the afternoon the whole of the women and children, all the sick and wounded, in every conceivable kind of conveyance, were in full retreat towards Cawnpore. General Outram's Division being made up to four thousand men was left in the Alambagh to hold the enemy in check, and to show them that Lucknow was not abandoned, while three thousand fighting men, to guard over two thousand women and children, sick and wounded, commenced their march southwards. So far as I can remember the Third and Fifth Punjab Infantry formed the infantry of the advance-guard; the Ninth Lancers and Horse Artillery supplied the flanking parties; while the rear guard, being the post of honour, was given to the Ninety-Third, a troop of the Ninth Lancers and Bourchier's light field-battery, No. 17 of the Honourable East India Company's artillery. We started from the Alambagh late in the afternoon, and reached Bunni Bridge, seventeen miles from Lucknow, about 11 p.m. Here the regiment halted till daylight on the morning of the 28th of November, but the advance-guard with the women and children, sick and wounded, had been moving since 2 a.m.

All the subaltern officers in my company were wounded, and I was told off, with a guard of about twenty men, to see all the baggage-carts across Bunni Bridge and on their way to Cawnpore. While I was on this duty an amusing incident happened. A commissariat cart, a common country hackery loaded with biscuits, got upset, and its wheel broke just as we were moving it on to the road. The only person near it belonging to the Commissariat Department was a young *babu** named Hira Lal Chatterjee, a boy of about seventeen or eighteen years of age, who defended his charge as long as he could, but he was soon put on one side, the biscuits-bags were ripped open, and the men commenced filling their

* Clerk. [M.E.]

haversacks from them. Just at this time, an escort of the Ninth Lancers, with some staff-officers, rode up from the rear. It was the Commander-in-Chief and his staff. Hira Lal seeing him rushed up and called out: 'O my Lord, you are my father and my mother! what shall I tell you! These wild Highlanders will not hear me, but are stealing commissariat biscuits like fine fun.' Sir Colin pulled up, and asked the *babu* if there was no officer present; to which Hira Lal replied, 'No officer, sir, only one corporal, and he tell me, "Shut up, or I'll shoot you, same like rebel mutineer!"' Hearing this I stepped out of the crowd and saluting Sir Colin, told him that all the officers of my company were wounded except Captain Dawson, who was in front; that I and a party of men had been left to see the last of the carts on to the road; that this cart had broken down, and as there was no other means of carrying the biscuits, the men had filled their haversacks with them rather than leave them on the ground. On hearing that, Hira Lal again came to the front with clasped hands, saying: 'O my Lord, if one cart of biscuits short, Major Fitzgerald not listen to me, but will order thirty lashes with provost-marshal's cat! What can a poor *babu* do with such wild Highlanders?' Sir Colin replied: 'Yes *babu*, I know these Highlanders are very wild fellows when hungry; let them have the biscuits;' and turning to one of the staff, he directed him to give a voucher to the *babu* that a cart loaded with biscuits had broken down and the contents had been divided among the rear-guard by order of the Commander-in-Chief. Sir Colin then turned to us and said: 'Men, I give you the biscuits; divide them with your comrades in front; but you must promise me should a cart loaded with rum break down, you will not interfere with it.' We all replied: 'No, no, Sir Colin, if rum breaks down we'll not touch it.' 'All right,' said Sir Colin, 'remember I trust you,' and looking round he said, 'I know every one of you,' and rode on. We very soon found room for the biscuits, until we got up to the rest of the company, when we honestly shared them.

About five miles farther on a general halt was made for a short rest and for all stragglers to come up. Sir Colin himself, being still with the column, ordered the Ninety-Third to form up, and, calling the officers to the front, he made the first announcement to the regiment that General Wyndham had been attacked by the Nana Sahib and the Gwalior Contingent* in Cawnpore; that his force

* See Introduction, p. 7. [M.E.]

had been obliged to retire within the fort at the head of the bridge
of boats, and that we must reach Cawnpore that night, because, if
the bridge of boats should be captured before we got there, we
would be cut off in Oudh with fifty thousand of our enemies in our
rear, a well-equipped army of forty thousand men, with a powerful
train of artillery numbering over forty siege guns, in our front, and
with all the women and children, sick and wounded, to guard. 'So,
Ninety-Third,' said the grand old Chief, 'I don't ask you to under-
take this forced march, in your present tired condition, without
good reason. You must reach Cawnpore tonight at all costs.' And,
as usual, when he took the men into his confidence, he was
answered from the ranks, 'All right, Sir Colin, we'll do it.' To
which he replied, 'Very well, Ninety-Third, remember I depend
on you.' And he and his staff and escort rode on.

By this time we could plainly hear the guns of the Gwalior Contingent bombarding General Wyndham's position in Cawnpore;
and although terribly footsore and tired, not having had our clothes
off, nor a change of socks, since the 10th of the month (now eighteen days) we trudged on our weary march, every mile making the
roar of the guns in front more audible. I may remark here that
there is nothing to rouse tired soldiers like a good cannonade in
front; it is the best tonic out! Even the youngest soldier who has
once been under fire, and can distinguish the sound of a shotted
gun from blank, pricks up his ears at the sound and steps out with
a firmer tread and a more erect bearing.

I shall never forget the misery of that march! However, we
reached the sands on the banks of the Ganges, on the Oudh side of
the river opposite Cawnpore, just as the sun was setting, having
covered the forty-seven miles under thirty hours. Of course the
great hardship of the march was caused by our worn-out state after
eighteen days' continual duty, without a change of clothes or our
accoutrements off. And when we got in sight of Cawnpore, the
first thing we saw was the enemy on the opposite side of the river
from us, making bonfires of our spare kits and baggage which had
been left at Cawnpore when we advanced for the relief of Lucknow!
Tired as we were, we assisted to drag Peel's heavy guns into
position on the banks of the river, whence the Blue-jackets opened
fire on the left flank of the enemy, the bonfires of our spare baggage
being a fine mark for them.

Just as the Nana Sahib had got his first gun to bear on the

bridge of boats, that gun was struck on the side by one of Peel's 24-pounders and upset, and an 8-inch shell from one of his howitzers bursting in the midst of a crowd of them, we could see them bolting helter-skelter. This put a stop to their game for the night, and we lay down and rested on the sands till daybreak next morning, the 29th of November.

I must mention here an experience of my own which I always recall to mind when I read some of the insane ravings of the Anti-Opium Society against the use of that drug. I was so completely tired out by that terrible march that after I had lain down for about half an hour I positively could not stand up, I was so stiff and worn out. Having been on duty as orderly corporal before leaving the Alambagh, I had been much longer on my feet than the rest of the men; in fact, I was tired out before we started on our march on the afternoon of the 27th, and now, after having covered forty-seven miles under thirty hours, my condition can be better imagined than described. After I became cold, I grew so stiff that I positively could not use my legs. Now Captain Dawson had a native servant, an old man named Hyder Khan, who had been an officers' servant all his life, and had been through many campaigns. I had made a friend of old Hyder before we left Chinsurah, and he did not forget me. Having ridden the greater part of the march on the camel carrying his master's baggage, Hyder was comparatively fresh when he got into camp, and about the time our canteen-sergeant got up and was calling for orderly-corporals to draw grog for the men, old Hyder came looking for me, and when he saw my tired state, he said, in his camp English: 'Corporal *sahib*, you God-damn tired; don't drink grog. Old Hyder give you something damn much better than grog for tired mans.' With that he went away, but shortly after returned, and gave me a small pill, which he told me was opium, and about half a pint of hot tea, which he had pre-pared for himself and his master. I swallowed the pill and drank the tea, and *in less than ten minutes* I felt myself so much refreshed as to be able to get up and draw the grog for the men of the company and to serve it out to them while the colour-sergeant called the roll. I then lay down, rolled up in my sepoy officer's quilt, which I had carried from the Shah Najaf, and had a sound refreshing sleep till next morning, and then got up so much restored that, except for the sores on my feet from broken blisters, I could have undertaken another forty-mile march. I always recall this experience when I read many of the ignorant arguments of the Anti-Opium Society, who would, if they had the power, compel the Government to deprive every hard-worked *coolie* of the only solace in his life of toil. I am certainly not an opium-eater, and the abuse of opium may be injurious, as is the abuse of anything; but I am so convinced in my own mind of the beneficial effects of the temperate use of the drug, that if I were the general of an army after a forced march like that of the retreat from Lucknow to the relief of Cawnpore, I would make the Medical Department give every man a pill of opium and half a pint of hot tea, instead of rum or liquor of any sort! I hate drunkenness as much as anybody, but I have no sympathy with what I may call the intemperate temperance of most of our tee-totallers and the Anti-Opium Society. My experience has been as great and as varied as that of most Europeans in India, and that experience has led me to the conviction that the members of the Anti-Opium Society are either culpably ignorant of facts, or dishonest in the way they represent what they wish others to believe to be facts. Most of the assertions made about the Government connection with opium being a hindrance to mission-work and the spread of Christianity, are gross exaggerations not borne out by experience, and the opium slave and the opium den, as depicted in much of the literature on this subject, have no existence except in the distorted imagination of the writers.

Early on the morning of the 29th of November the Ninety-Third crossed the bridge of boats, and it was well that Sir Colin had returned so promptly from Lucknow to the relief of Cawnpore, for General Wyndham's troops were not only beaten and cowed— they were utterly demoralised.

When the Commander-in-Chief left Cawnpore for Lucknow, General Wyndham, known as the 'Hero of the Redan'*, had been left in command at Cawnpore with instructions to strengthen his position by every means, and to detain all detachments arriving from Calcutta after the 10th of November, because it was known that the Gwalior Contingent were in great force somewhere across the Jumna, and there was every probability that they would either attack Cawnpore, or cross into Oudh to fall on the rear of the Commander-in-Chief's force and prevent the relief of Lucknow. But strict orders were given to General Wyndham that he was *on no account* to move out of Cawnpore, should the Gwalior Con-

* An episode in the Crimean War. [M.E.]

tingent advance on his position, but to act on the defensive, and to hold his entrenchments and guard the bridge of boats at all hazards. By that time the entrenchment or mud fort at the Cawnpore end of the bridge had become a place of considerable strength under the able direction of Captain Mowbray Thomson, one of the four survivors of General Wheeler's force. Captain Thomson had over four thousand *coolies* daily employed on the defences from daybreak till dark, and he was a most energetic officer himself, so that by the time we passed through Cawnpore for the relief of Lucknow this position had become quite a strong fortification, especially when compared with the miserable apology for an entrenchment so gallantly defended by General Wheeler's small force and won from him by such black treachery. When we advanced for the relief of Lucknow, all our spare baggage, five hundred new tents, and a great quantity of clothing for the troops coming down from Delhi, were shut up in Cawnpore with a large quantity of spare ammunition, harness, and saddlery; in brief, property to the value of over five *lakhs** of rupees was left stored in the church and in the houses which were still standing near the church between the town and the river, a short distance from the house in which the women and children were murdered. All this property, as already mentioned, fell into the hands of the Gwalior Contingent, and we returned just in time to see them making bonfires of what they could not use. Colonel Sir Robert Napier lost all the records of his long service, and many valuable engineering papers which could never be replaced. As for us of the Ninety-Third, we lost all our spare kits, and were now without a chance of a change of underclothing or socks. Let all who may read this consider what it meant to us, who had not changed our clothes from the 10th of the month, and now, on the morning of the 29th, saw the enemy making bonfires of our kits, just as we were within reach of them. It was hardly soothing to contemplate.

But to return to General Wyndham's force. By the 26th of November it had numbered two thousand four hundred men, and when he heard of the advance of the Nana Sahib at the head of the Gwalior Contingent, Wyndham considered himself strong enough to disobey the orders of the Commander-in-Chief, and moved out of his entrenchment to give them battle, encountering their advance guard about seven miles from Cawnpore. He at once attacked and

* 500,000. [M.E.]

drove it back through a village in its rear; but behind the village he found himself confronted by an army of over forty thousand men, twenty-five thousand of them being the famous Gwalior Contingent, the best disciplined troops in India, which had never been beaten and considered themselves invincible, and which, in addition to a siege train of thirty heavy guns, 24 and 32-pounders, had a well-appointed and well-drilled field-artillery. General Wyndham now saw his mistake, and gave the order for retreat. His small force retired in good order, and encamped on the plain outside Cawnpore on the Bithur road for the night, to find itself outflanked and almost surrounded by Tantia Topi and his Mara-thas on the morning of the 27th; and at the end of five hours' fighting a general retreat into the fort had again to be ordered.

The retiring force was overwhelmed by a murderous cannonade, and, being largely composed of young soldiers, a panic ensued. The men got out of hand, and fled for the fort with a loss of over three hundred—mostly killed, because the wounded who fell into the hands of the enemy were cut to pieces—and several guns. The Rev Mr Moore, Church of England Chaplain with General Wyndham's force, gave a very sad picture of the panic in which the men fled for the fort, and his description was borne out by what I saw myself when we passed through the fort on the morning of the 29th. Mr Moore said: 'The men got quite out of hand and fled pell-mell for the fort. An old Sikh officer at the gate tried to stop them, and to form them up in some order, and when they pushed him aside and rushed past him, he lifted up his hands and said, "You are not the brothers of the men who beat the Khalsa army and conquered the Punjab!" ' Mr Moore went on to say 'The old Sikh followed the flying men through the Fort Gate, and patting some of them on the back said, "Don't run, don't be afraid, there is nothing to hurt you!" '

The fact is the men were mostly young soldiers, belonging to many different regiments, simply battalions of detachments. They were crushed by the heavy and well-served artillery of the enemy, and if the truth must be told, they had no confidence in their com-mander, who was a brave soldier, but no general; so when the men were once seized with panic, there was no stopping them. The only regiment, or rather part of a regiment (for they only numbered fourteen officers of all ranks and a hundred and sixty men) which behaved well, was the old Sixty-Fourth, and two companies of the

Thirty-Fourth and Eighty-Second, making up a weak battalion of barely three hundred. This was led by brave old Brigadier Wilson, who held them in hand until he brought them forward to cover the retreat, which he did with a loss of seven officers killed and two wounded, eighteen men of the Sixty-Fourth killed and twenty-five wounded, with equally heavy proportions killed and wounded from the companies of the Thirty-Fourth and Eighty-Second. Brigadier Wilson first had his horse shot, and was then himself killed, while urging the men to maintain the honour of the regiment. The command then devolved on Major Stirling, one of the Sixty-Fourth, who was cut down in the act of spiking one of the enemy's guns, and Captain M'Crea of the same regiment was also cut down just as he had spiked his fourth gun. This charge, and these individual acts of bravery, retarded the advance of the enemy till some sort of order had been re-established inside the fort. The Sixty-Fourth were then driven back, and obliged to leave their dead.

This then was the state of matters when we reached Cawnpore from Lucknow. The whole of our spare baggage was captured: the city of Cawnpore and the whole of the river-side up to the house where the Nana had slaughtered the women and children were in the hands of the enemy; but they had not yet injured the bridge of boats, nor crossed the canal, and the road to Allahabad still remained open.

We crossed the bridge without any loss except one officer, who was slightly wounded by being struck on the shin by a spent bullet from a charge of grape. He was a long slender youth of about sixteen or seventeen years of age, whom the men had named 'Jack Straw'. He was knocked down, just as we cleared the bridge of boats, among the blood of some camp-followers who had been killed by the bursting of a shell just in front of us. Sergeant Paton, of my company, picked him up, and put him into an empty *dooly* which was passing.

During the day a piquet of one sergeant, one corporal, and about twenty men, under command of Lieutenant Stirling, who was afterwards killed on the 5th of December, was sent out to bring in the body of Brigadier Wilson. A man named Doran, of the Sixty-Fourth, who had gone up to Lucknow in the Volunteer Cavalry, and had there done good service and returned with our force, volunteered to go out with them to identify the brigadier's body,

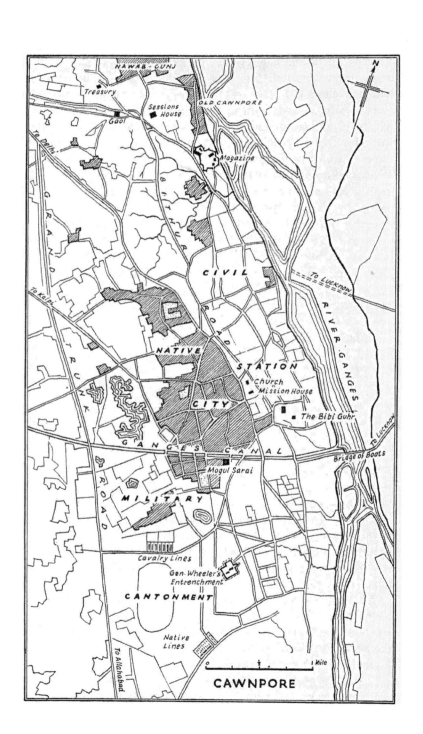

NAWAB - GUNJ

Treasury

OLD CAWNPORE

Sessions
House

Gaol

To Delhi

Magazine

CIVIL

To Lucknow

To Kalpi

NATIVE

STATION

Church
Mission House

CITY

The Bibi Guhr

To Lucknow

GANGES CANAL

Bridge of Boats

Mogul Sarai

MILITARY

ROAD

Cavalry Lines

Gen. Wheeler's
Entrenchment

CANTONMENT

Native
Lines

0   ½   1 Mile

CAWNPORE

because there were many more killed near the same place, and their corpses having been stripped, they could not be identified by their uniform, and it would have been impossible to have brought in all without serious loss. The party reached the brigadier's body without apparently attracting the attention of the enemy; but just as two men, Rule of my regiment and Patrick Doran, were lifting it into the *dooly* they were seen, and the enemy opened fire on them. A bullet struck Doran and went right through his body from side to side, without touching any of the vital organs, just as he was bending down to lift the brigadier—a most extraordinary wound! If the bullet had deviated a hair's-breadth to either side, the wound must have been mortal, but Doran was able to walk back to the fort.

During the time that this piquet was engaged, the Blue-jackets of Peel's Brigade and our heavy artillery had taken up positions in front of the fort, and showed the gunners of the Gwalior Contingent that they were no longer confronted by raw inexperienced troops. By the afternoon of the 29th of November, the whole of the women and children and sick and wounded from Lucknow had crossed the Ganges, and encamped behind the Ninety-Third on the Allahabad road, and here I will leave them and close this chapter.

8. THE NANA SAHIB'S TREASURE

So far as I remember, the 30th of November, 1857, passed without any movement on the part of the enemy, and the Commander-in-Chief, in his letter describing the state of affairs to the Governor-General, said, 'I am obliged to submit to the hostile occupation of Cawnpore until the actual despatch of all my incumbrances towards Allahabad is effected.' St Andrew's day and evening passed without molestation, except that strong piquets lined the canal and guarded our left and rear from surprise, and the men in camp slept accoutred, ready to turn out at the least alarm. But during the night, or early on the morning of the 1st of December, the enemy had quietly advanced some guns, unseen by our piquets, right up to the Cawnpore side of the canal, and suddenly opened fire on the Ninety-Third just as we were falling in for muster-parade, sending round-shot and shell right through our tents. One shrapnel shell burst right in the centre of Captain Cornwall's company severely wounding the captain, Colour-Sergeant M'Intyre, and five men, but not killing anyone.

Captain Cornwall was the oldest officer in the regiment, even an older soldier than Colonel Leith-Hay who had then commanded it for over three years, and for long he had been named by the men 'Old Daddy Cornwall'. He was poor, and had been unable to purchase promotion, and in consequence was still a captain with over thirty-five years' service. The bursting of the shell right over his head stunned the old gentleman, and a bullet went through his shoulder, breaking his collar-bone and cutting a deep furrow down his back. The old man was rather stout and very short-sighted; the shock of the fall stunned him for some time, and before he regained his senses Dr Munro had cut the bullet out of his back and bandaged up his wound as well as possible. Daddy came to himself just as the men were lifting him into a *dooly*. Seeing Dr Munro standing by with the bullet in his hand, about to present it to him as a memento of Cawnpore, Daddy gasped out, 'Munro, is my wound dangerous?' 'No, Cornwall,' was the answer, 'not if you don't excite yourself into a fever; you will get over it all right.' The next question put was, 'Is the road clear to Allahabad?' To which

Munro replied that it was, and that he hoped to have all the sick and wounded sent down country within a day or two. 'Then by ——' said Daddy, with considerable emphasis, 'I'm off.' The poor old fellow had through long disappointment become like our soldiers in Flanders—he sometimes swore; but considering how promotion had passed over him, that was perhaps excusable.*

But I must return to my story. Being shelled out of our tents, the regiment was advanced to the side of the canal under cover of the mud walls of what had formerly been the sepoy lines, in which we took shelter from the fire of the enemy. Later in the day Colonel Ewart lost his left arm by a round-shot striking him on the elbow just as he had dismounted from his charger on his return from visiting the piquets on the left and rear of our position, he being the field-officer for the day. This caused universal regret in the regiment; Ewart being the most popular officer in it.

By the evening of the 3rd of December the whole of the women and children, and as many of the wounded as could bear to be moved, were on their way to Allahabad; and during the 4th and 5th reinforcements reached Cawnpore from England, among them our old comrades of the Forty-Second whom we had left at Dover in May. We were right glad to see them, on the morning of the 5th December, marching in with bagpipes playing, which was the first intimation we had of another Highland regiment being near us. These reinforcements raised the force under Sir Colin Campbell to five thousand infantry, six hundred cavalry, and thirty-five guns.

Early on the morning of the 6th of December we struck our tents, which we loaded on elephants, and marched to a place of safety behind the fort on the river bank, where we formed up in rear of the unroofed barracks—the Forty-Second, Fifty-Third, Ninety-Third, and Fourth Punjab Infantry, with Peel's Brigade and several batteries of artillery, among them Colonel Bourchier's light field-battery (No. 17 of the old Company's European artillery), a most daring lot of fellows, the Ninth Lancers, and one squadron of Hodson's Horse under command of Lieutenant Gough, a worthy pupil of a famous master. This detachment of Hodson's Horse had come down with Sir Hope Grant from Delhi, and served

* Daddy Cornwall went home in the same vessel as a rich widow, whom he married on arrival in Dublin, his native place, the corporation of which presented him with a valuable sword and the freedom of the city. The death of Brigadier-General Hope in the following April gave Captain Cornwall his majority without purchase, and he returned to India in the end of 1859 to command the regiment.

at the final relief of Lucknow and the retreat to the succour of
Cawnpore. The headquarters of the regiment under its famous
commander had been left with Brigadier Showers.

As this force was formed up in columns, masked from the view
of the enemy by the barracks on the plain of Cawnpore, the Commander-in-Chief rode up, and told us that he had just got a
telegram informing him of the safe arrival of the women and
children, sick and wounded, at Allahabad, and that now we were to
give battle to the famous Gwalior Contingent, consisting of
twenty-five thousand well-disciplined troops, with about ten thousand of the Nana Sahib's Marathas and all the *badmashes* of
Cawnpore, Kalpi, and Gwalior, under command of the Nana in
person, who had proclaimed himself Peshwa and Chief of the
Maratha power, with Tantia Topi, Bala Sahib (the Nana's
brother), and Raja Koer Singh as divisional commanders, and with
all the native officers of the Gwalior Contingent as brigade and
regimental commanders. Sir Colin also warned us that there was a
large quantity of rum in the enemy's camp, which we must carefully avoid, because it was reported to have been drugged. 'But,
Ninety-Third,' he continued, 'I trust you. The supernumerary rank
will see that no man breaks the ranks, and I have ordered the rum
to be destroyed as soon as the camp is taken.'

The Chief then rode on to the other regiments and as soon as he
had addressed a short speech to each, a signal was sent up from
Peel's rocket battery, and General Wyndham opened the ball on his
side with every gun at his disposal, attacking the enemy's left
between the city and the river. Sir Colin himself led the advance,
the Fifty-Third and Fourth Punjab Infantry in skirmishing order,
with the Ninety-Third in line, the cavalry on our left, and Peel's
guns and the horse-artillery at intervals, with the Forty-Second
in the second line for our support.

Directly we emerged from the shelter of the buildings which had
masked our formation, the piquets fell back, the skirmishers
advanced at the double, and the enemy opened a tremendous
cannonade on us with round-shot, shell, and grape. But, nothing
daunted, our skirmishers soon lined the canal, and our line
advanced, with the pipers playing and the colours in front of the
centre company, without the least wavering—except now and then
opening out to let through the round-shot which were falling in
front, and rebounding along the hard ground—determined to show

the Gwalior Contingent that they had different men to meet from those whom they had encountered under Wyndham a week before. By the time we had reached the canal, Peel's Blue-jackets were calling out 'Damn these cow horses'—meaning the gun-bullocks—'they're too slow! Come, you Ninety-Third, give us a hand with the drag-ropes as you did at Lucknow!' We were then well under the range of the enemy's guns, and the excitement was at its height. A company of the Ninety-Third slung their rifles, and dashed to the assistance of the Blue-jackets. The bullocks were cast adrift, and the native drivers were not slow in going to the rear. The drag-ropes were manned, and the 24-pounders wheeled abreast of the first line of skirmishers just as if they had been light field-pieces.

When we reached the bank the infantry paused for a moment to see if the canal could be forded or if we should have to cross by the bridge over which the light field-battery were passing at the gallop, unlimbering and opening fire as soon as they cleared the head of the bridge, to protect our advance. At this juncture the enemy opened on us with grape and canister shot, but they fired high and did us but little damage. As the peculiar *whish* (a sound when once heard is never to be forgotten) of the grape was going over our heads, the Blue-jackets gave a ringing cheer for the 'Red, white, and blue!' While the Ninety-Third, led off by Sergeant Daniel White, struck up *The Battle of the Alma*, a song composed in the Crimea by Corporal John Brown of the Grenadier Guards, and often sung round the camp-fires in front of Sebastopol.

Around our bivouac fires that night as *The Battle of the Alma* was sung again, Daniel White told us that when the Blue-jackets commenced cheering under the hail of grape-shot, he remembered that the Scots Greys and Ninety-Second Highlanders had charged at Waterloo singing Bruce's address at Bannockburn, *Scots wha hae*, and trying to think of something equally appropriate in which Peel's Brigade might join, he could not at the moment recall anything better than the old Crimean song aforesaid.

After clearing the canal and reforming our ranks, we came under shelter of a range of brick kilns behind which stood the camp of the enemy, and behind the camp their infantry were drawn up in columns, not deployed in line. The rum against which Sir Colin had warned us was in front of the camp, casks standing on end with the heads knocked out for convenience; and there is no doubt but the enemy expected the Europeans would break their ranks when they saw the rum, and had formed up their columns to fall on us in the event of such a contingency. But the Ninety-Third marched right on past the rum barrels, and the supernumerary rank soon upset the casks, leaving the contents to soak into the dry ground.

As soon as we cleared the camp, our line of infantry was halted. Up to that time, except the·skirmishers, we had not fired a shot, and we could not understand the reason of the halt till we saw the Ninth Lancers and the detachment of Hodson's Horse galloping round some fields of tall sugar-cane on the left, masking the light field-battery. When the enemy saw the tips of the lances (they evidently did not see the guns) they quickly formed squares of brigades. They were armed with the old musket, 'Brown Bess', and did not open fire till the cavalry were within about three hundred yards. Just as they commenced to fire, we could hear Sir Hope Grant, in a voice as loud as a trumpet, give the command to the cavalry, 'Squadrons, outwards!' while Bourchier gave the order to his gunners, 'Action, front!' The cavalry wheeled as if they had been at a review on the Calcutta parade-ground; the guns, having previously been charged with grape, were swung round, un-limbered as quick as lightning within about two hundred and fifty yards of the squares, and round after round of grape was poured into the enemy with murderous effect, every charge going right through, leaving a lane of dead from four to five yards wide. By this time our line was advanced close up behind the battery, and we could see the mounted officers of the enemy, as soon as they caught sight of the guns, dash out of the squares and fly like light-ning across the plain. Directly the squares were broken, our cavalry charged, while the infantry advanced at the double with the bayo-net. The battle was won, and the famous Gwalior Contingent was a flying rabble, although the struggle was protracted in a series of hand-to-hand fights all over the plain, no quarter being given. Peel's guns were wheeled up, as already mentioned, as if they had been 6-pounders, and the left wing of the enemy taken in rear and their retreat on the Kalpi road cut off. What escaped of their right wing fled along this road. The cavalry and horse-artillery led by Sir Colin Campbell in person, the whole of the Fifty-Third, the Fourth Punjab Infantry, and two companies of the Ninety-Third, pursued the flying mass for fourteen miles. The rebels, being cut down by hundreds wherever they attempted to rally for a stand,

—nothing! We had even to pay from our own pockets for the replacement of our kits which were taken by the Gwalior Contingent when they captured Wyndham's camp.

By Christmas Day, 1857, we had recovered all the gold and silver plate of the ex-Peshwa and the thirty *lakhs* of treasure from the well in Bithur, and on the morning of the 27th we marched for the recapture of Fatehgarh which was held by a strong force under the Nawab of Farruckabad. But I must leave the reoccupation of Fatehgarh for another chapter.

9. THE GRAND TRUNK ROAD

As a further proof that the British star was now in the ascendant, before we had been many days in Bithur each company had got its full complement of native establishment, such as cooks, water-carriers, washermen, etc. We left Bithur on the 27th of December *en route* for Fatehgarh, and on the 28th we made a forced march of twenty-five miles, joining the Commander-in-Chief on the 29th. Early on the 30th we reached a place named Meerun-ke-serai, and our tents had barely been pitched when word went through the camp like wildfire that Hodson, of Hodson's Horse, and another officer had arrived in camp with despatches from Brigadier Seaton to the Commander-in-Chief, having ridden from Mainpuri, about seventy miles from where we were.

We of the Ninety-Third were eager to see Hodson, having heard so much about him from the men of the Ninth Lancers. There was nothing, however daring or difficult, that Hodson was not believed capable of doing, and a ride of seventy miles more or less through a country swarming with enemies, where every European who ventured beyond the range of British guns literally carried his life in his hand, was not considered anything extraordinary for him. Personally, I was most anxious to see this famous fellow, but as yet there was no chance; Hodson was in the tent of the Commander-in-Chief, and no one knew when he might come out. However, the hours passed, and during the afternoon a man of my company rushed into the tent, calling, 'Come, boys, and see Hodson! He and Sir Colin are in front of the camp; Sir Colin is showing him round, and the smile on the old Chief's face shows how he appreciates his companion.' I hastened to the front of the camp, and was rewarded by having a good look at Hodson; and, as the man who had called us had said, I could see that he had made a favourable impression on Sir Colin. Little did I then think that in less than three short months I should see Hodson receive his death-wound.

On the 1st of January, 1858, our force reached the Kali Nadi suspension bridge near Kudagunj, about fifteen miles from Fatehgarh, just in time to prevent the total destruction of the bridge by

View of Lucknow

the enemy, who had removed a good part of the planking from the roadway, and had commenced to cut the ironwork when we arrived. We halted on the Cawnpore side of the Kali Nadi on New Year's Day, while the engineers, under cover of strong piquets, were busy replacing the planking of the roadway on the suspension bridge. Early on the morning of the 2nd of January the enemy from Fatehgarh, under cover of a thick fog along the valley of the Kali Nadi, came down in great force to dispute the passage of the river. The first intimation of their approach was a shell fired on our advance piquet; but our camp was close to the bridge, and the whole force was under arms in an instant. As soon as the fog lifted the enemy were seen to have occupied the village of Kudagunj in great force, and to have advanced one gun, a 24-pounder, planting it in the toll-house which commanded the passage of the bridge, so as to fire it out of the front window just as if from the porthole of a ship.

As soon as the position of the enemy was seen, the cavalry brigade of our force was detached to the left, under cover of the dense jungle along the river, to cross by a ford which was discovered about five miles up stream to our left, the intention of the movement being to get in behind the enemy and cut off his retreat to Fatehgarh.

The Fifty-Third were pushed across the bridge to reinforce the piquets, with orders not to advance, but to act on the defensive, so as to allow time for the cavalry to get behind the enemy. The right wing of the Ninety-Third was also detached with some horse-artillery guns to the right, to cross by another ford about three miles below the bridge, to attack the enemy on his left flank. The left wing was held in reserve with the remainder of the force behind the bridge, to be in readiness to reinforce the Fifty-Third in case of need.

By the time these dispositions were made, the enemy's gun from the toll-house had begun to do considerable damage. Peel's heavy guns were accordingly brought to bear on it, and, after a round or two to feel their distance, they were able to pitch an 8-inch shell right through the window, which burst under the gun, upsetting it, and killing or disabling most of the enemy in the house.

Immediately after this the Fifty-Third, being well in advance, noticed the enemy attempting to withdraw some of his heavy guns from the village, and disregarding the order of the Commander-in-Chief not to precipitate the attack, they charged these guns and captured two or three of them. This check caused the enemy's line to retire, and Sir Colin himself rode up to the Fifty-Third to bring to book the officer commanding them for prematurely commencing the action. This officer threw the blame on the men, stating that they had made the charge against his orders, and that the officers had been unable to keep them back. Sir Colin then turned on the men, threatening to send them to the rear, and to make them do fatigue-duty and baggage-guard for the rest of the campaign. On this an old Irishman from the ranks called out: 'Sure, Sir Colin, you don't mean it! You'll never send us on fatigue-duty because we captured those guns that the Pandies were carrying off?' Hearing this, Sir Colin asked what guns he meant. 'Shure, them's the guns,' was the answer, 'that Sergeant Dobbin [Joe Lee] and his section are dragging on to the road.' Sir Colin seeing the guns, his stern countenance relaxed and broke into a smile, and he made some remark to the officer commanding that he did not know about the guns having been withdrawn before the regiment had made the rush on the enemy. On this the Irish spokesman from the ranks called out: 'Three cheers for the Commander-in-Chief, boys! I told you he did not mean us to let the Pandies carry off those guns.'

By this time our right wing and the horse-artillery had crossed the ford on our right and were well advanced on the enemy's left flank. But we of the main line, composed of the Eighth, the Forty-Second, Fifty-Third, and left wing of the Ninety-Third under Adrian Hope, were allowed to advance slowly, just keeping them in sight. The enemy retired in an orderly manner for about three or four miles, when they formed up to make a stand, evidently thinking we were afraid to press them too closely. As soon as they faced round again, our line was halted only about seven hundred yards from them, and just then we could see our cavalry debouching on to the Grand Trunk Road about a mile from where we were. My company was in the centre of the road, and I could see the tips of the lances of the Ninth wheeling into line for a charge right in the enemy's rear. He was completely out-generalled, and his retreat cut off.

The excitement was just then intense, as we dared not fire for fear of hitting our men in the rear. The Forty-First Native Infantry was the principal regiment of the enemy's line on the Grand Trunk

Road. Directly they saw the Lancers in their rear they formed square while the enemy's cavalry charged our men, but were met in fine style by Hodson's Horse and sent flying across the fields in all directions. The Ninth came down on the square of the Native infantry, who stood their ground and opened fire. The Lancers charged well up to within about thirty yards, when the horses turned off right and left from the solid square. We were just preparing to charge it with the bayonet, when at that moment the squadrons were brought round again, just as a hawk takes a circle for a swoop on its prey, and we saw Sergeant-Major May, who was mounted on a powerful but untrained horse, dash on the square and leap right into it, followed by the squadron on that side. The square being thus broken, the other troops of the Ninth rode into the flying mass, and in less than five minutes the Forty-First regiment of Native Infantry was wiped out of the ranks of the mutineers. The enemy's line of retreat became a total rout, and the plain for miles was strewn with corpses speared down by the Lancers or hewn down by the keen-edged sabres of Hodson's Horse.

Our infantry line now advanced, but there was nothing for us to do but collect the ammunition-carts and baggage of the enemy. Just about sunset we halted and saw the Lancers and Sikhs returning with the captured standards and every gun which the enemy had brought into the field in the morning. The infantry formed up along the side of the Grand Trunk Road to cheer the cavalry as they returned. It was a sight never to be forgotten—the infantry and sailors cheering the Lancers and Sikhs, and the latter returning our cheers and waving the captured standards and their lances and sabres over their heads! Sir Colin Campbell rode up, and lifting his hat, thanked the Ninth Lancers and Sikhs for their day's work. It was reported in the camp that Sir Hope Grant had recommended Sergeant-Major May for the Victoria Cross, but that May had modestly remonstrated against the honour, saying that every man in the Ninth was as much entitled to the Cross as he was, and that he was only able to break the square by the accident of being mounted on an untrained horse which charged into the square instead of turning off from it. This is of course hearsay, but I believe it is fact.

We reached Fatehgarh on the morning of the 3rd of January to find it deserted, the enemy having got such a 'drubbing' that it had struck terror into their reserves, which had bolted across the Ganges, leaving large quantities of Government property behind them, consisting of tents and all the ordnance stores of the Gun-carriage Agency. The enemy had also established a gun and shot and shell foundry here, and a powder-factory, all of which they had abandoned, leaving a number of brass guns in the lathes, half turned, with many more just cast, and large quantities of metal and material for the manufacture of both powder and shot.

During the afternoon of the day of our arrival the whole force was turned out, owing to a report that the Nawab of Farruckabad was still in the town; and it was said that the civil officer with the force had sent a proclamation through the city that it would be given over to plunder if the Nawab was not surrendered. Whether this was true or not, I cannot say. The district was no longer under martial law, as from the date of the defeat of the Gwalior Con-tingent the civil power had resumed authority on the right bank of the Ganges. But so far as the country was concerned, around Fatehgarh at least, this merely meant that the hangman's noose was to be substituted for rifle-bullet and bayonet. However, our force had scarcely been turned out to threaten the town of Farrucka-bad when the Nawab was brought out, bound hand and foot, and carried by *coolies* on a common country *charpoy*.* I don't know what process of trial he underwent; but I fear he had neither jury nor counsel, and I know that he was first smeared over with pig's fat, flogged by sweepers, and then hanged. This was by the orders of the civil commissioner. Both Sir Colin Campbell and Sir William Peel were said to have protested against the barbarity, but this I don't know for certain.

We halted in Fatehgarh till the 6th, on which date a brigade composed of the Forty-Second, Ninety-Third, a regiment of Pun-jab infantry, a battery of artillery, a squadron of the Ninth Lancers, and Hodson's Horse, marched to Palamhow in the Shamshabad district. This town had been a hot-bed of rebellion under the leadership of a former native collector of revenue, who had pro-claimed himself Raja of the district, and all the bad characters in it had flocked to his standard. However, the place was occupied with-out opposition. We encamped outside the town, and the civil police, along with the commissioner, arrested great numbers, among

* Bedstead.

them being the man who had proclaimed himself the Raja or Nawab for the King of Delhi. My company, with some of Hodson's Horse and two artillery guns, formed a guard for the civil commissioner in the *chowk* or principal square of the town. The commissioner held his court in what had formerly been the police station. I cannot say what form of trial the prisoners underwent, or what evidence was recorded against them. I merely know that they were marched up in batches, and shortly after marched back again to a large tree, which stood in the centre of the square, and hanged thereon. This went on from about three o'clock in the afternoon till daylight the following morning, when it was reported that there was no more room on the tree, and by that time there were one hundred and thirty men hanging from its branches. A grim spectacle indeed!

Many charges of cruelty and want of pity have been made against the character of Hodson. This makes me here mention a fact that certainly does not tend to prove these charges. During the afternoon of the day of which I write, Hodson visited the squadron of his regiment forming the cavalry of the civil commissioner's guard. Just at the time of his visit the commissioner wanted a hangman, and asked if any man of the Ninety-Third would volunteer for the job, stating as an inducement that all valuables in the way of rings or money found on the persons of the condemned would become the property of the executioner. No one volunteering for the job, the commissioner asked Jack Brian, a big tall fellow who was the right-hand man of the company, if he would act as executioner. Jack Brian turned round with a look of disgust, saying: 'Wha do ye tak' us for? We of the Ninety-Third enlisted to fight men with arms in their hands. I widna' become yer hangman for all the loot in India!' Captain Hodson was standing close by, and hearing the answer, said, 'Well answered, my brave fellow. I wish to shake hands with you,' which he did. Then turning to Captain Dawson, Hodson said: 'I'm sick of work of this kind. I'm glad I'm not on duty'; and he mounted his horse, and rode off. However, some *doms* or sweeper-police were found to act as hangmen, and the trials and executions proceeded.

We returned to Fatehgarh on the 12th of January and remained in camp there till the 26th, when another expedition was sent out in the same direction. But this time only the right wing of the Ninety-Third and a wing of the Forty-Second formed the infantry,

so my company remained in camp. This second force met with
more opposition than the first one. Lieutenant Macdowell,
Hodson's second in command, and several troopers were killed,
and Hodson himself and some of his men were badly wounded,
Hodson having two severe cuts on his sword arm; while the
infantry had several men. killed who were blown up with gunpowder. This force returned on the 28th of January, and either on
the 2nd or 3rd of February we left Fatehgarh *en route* again for
Lucknow *via* Cawnpore.

We reached Cawnpore by ordinary marches, crossed into Oudh,
and encamped at Unao till the whole of the siege-train was passed
on to Lucknow.

10. HISTORY OF A SPY

WHEN we returned to Cawnpore, although we had been
barely two months away, we found it much altered. Many of the
burnt-down bungalows were being rebuilt, and the fort at the end
of the bridge of boats had become quite a strong place. The well
where the murdered women and children were buried was now
completely filled up, and a wooden cross erected over it. I visited
the slaughter-house again, and found the walls of the several rooms
all scribbled over both in pencil and charcoal. This had been done
since my first visit in October; I am positive on this point. The
unfortunate women who were murdered in the house left no
writing on the walls whatever. There was writing on the walls of
the barrack-rooms of Wheeler's entrenchment, mostly notes that
had been made during the siege, but none on the walls of the
slaughter-house. As mentioned in my last chapter, we only halted
one day in Cawnpore before crossing into Oudh, and marching to
Unao about the 10th of February, we encamped there as a guard
for the siege-train and ordnance-park which was being pushed on
to Lucknow.

While at Unao a strange thing happened, which I shall here set
down. Men live such busy lives in India that many who may have
heard the story have possibly forgotten all about it, while to most
of my home-staying readers it will be quite fresh.

Towards the end of February, 1858, the army for the siege of
Lucknow was gradually being massed in front of the doomed city,
and lay, like a huge boa-constrictor coiled and ready for its spring,
all along the road from Cawnpore to the Alambagh. A strong
division, consisting of the Forty-Second and Ninety-Third Highlanders, the Fifty-Third, the Ninth Lancers, Peel's Naval Brigade,
the siege-train, and several batteries of field-artillery, with the
Fourth Punjab Infantry and other Punjabi corps, lay at Unao under
the command of General Sir Edward Lugard and Brigadier Adrian
Hope. We had been encamped in that place for about ten days—
the monotony of our lives being only occasionally broken by the
sound of distant cannonading in front—when we heard that General
Outram's position at the Alambagh had been vigorously attacked

by a force from Lucknow, sometimes led by the Maulvi,* and at others by the Begum† in person. Now and then somewhat duller sounds came from the rear, which, we understood, arose from the operations of Sir Robert Napier and his engineers, who were engaged in blowing up the temples of Siva and Kali overlooking the *ghats* at Cawnpore; not, as some have asserted, out of revenge, but for military considerations connected with the safety of the bridge of boats across the Ganges.

During one of these days of comparative inaction, I was lying in my tent reading some home papers which had just arrived by the mail, when I heard a man passing through the camp, calling out, 'Plum-cakes! plum-cakes! Very good plum-cakes! Taste and try before you buy!' The advent of a plum-cake *wallah* was an agreeable change from ration-beef and biscuit, and he was soon called into the tent, and his own maxim of 'taste and try before you buy' freely put into practice. This plum-cake vendor was a very good-looking, light-coloured native in the prime of life, dressed in scrupulously clean white clothes, with dark, curly whiskers and mustachios, carefully trimmed after the fashion of the Muhammadan native officers of John Company's‡ army. He had a well-developed forehead, a slightly aquiline nose, and intelligent eyes. Altogether his appearance was something quite different from that of the usual camp-follower. But his companion, or rather the man employed as *coolie* to carry his basket, was one of the most villainous-looking specimens of humanity I ever set eyes on. As was the custom in those days, seeing that he did not belong to our own bazaar, and being the non-commissioned officer in charge of the tent, I asked the plum-cake man if he was provided with a pass for visiting the camp? 'Oh yes, Sergeant *sahib*,' he replied, 'there's my pass all in order, not from the Brigade-Major, but from the Brigadier himself, the Honourable Adrian Hope. I'm Jamie Green, mess-*khansama*§ of the late (I forget the regiment he mentioned), and I have just come to Unao with a letter of introduction to General Hope from Sherer *sahib*, the magistrate and collector of Cawnpore. You will doubtless know General Hope's handwriting.' And there it was, all in order, authorising the bearer, by name

* Ahmad Ullah, the Maulvi of Faizabad, one of the leaders of the rebellion. [M.E.]
† Hazrat Mahal, one of the queens of the former King of Oudh, who had joined the rebels and whose son had been proclaimed king by them. [M.E.]
‡ The popular name for the East India Company. [M.E.]
§ Butler.

Jamie Green, etc. etc., to visit both the camp and outpost for the sale of his plum-cakes, in the handwriting of the brigadier, which was well known to all the non-commissioned officers of the Ninety-Third, Hope having been colonel of the regiment.

Next to his appearance what struck me as the most remarkable thing about Jamie Green was the purity and easy flow of his English, for he at once sat down beside me, and asked to see the newspapers, and seemed anxious to know what the English press said about the mutiny, and to talk of all subjects connected with the strength, etc., of the army, the preparations going forward for the siege of Lucknow, and how the newly-arrived regiments were likely to stand the hot weather. In course of conversation I made some remarks about the fluency of his English, and he accounted for it by stating that his father had been the mess-*khansama* of a European regiment, and that he had been brought up to speak English from his childhood, that he had learned to read and write in the regimental school, and for many years had filled the post of mess-writer, keeping all the accounts of the mess in English. During this time the men in the tent had been freely trying the plum-cakes, and a squabble arose between one of them and Jamie Green's servant about payment. When I made some remark about the villainous look of the latter Green replied: 'Oh, never mind him; he is an Irishman, and his name is Micky. His mother belongs to the regimental bazaar of the Eighty-Seventh Royal Irish, and he lays claim to the whole regiment, including the sergeant-major's cook, for his father. He has just come down from the Punjab with the Agra convoy, but the commanding officer dismissed him at Cawnpore, because he had a young wife of his own, and was jealous of the good looks of Micky. But,' continued Jamie Green, 'a joke is a joke, but to eat a man's plum-cakes and then refuse to pay for them must be a Highland joke!' On this every man in the tent, appreciating the good humour of Jamie Green, turned on the man who had refused payment, and he was obliged to fork out the amount demanded. Jamie Green and Micky passed on to another tent, after the former had borrowed a few of the latest of my newspapers. Thus ended my first interview with the plum-cake vendor.

The second one was more interesting, and with a sadder termination. On the evening of the day after the events just described, I was on duty as sergeant in charge of our camp rear-guard, and at sunset when the orderly-corporal came round with

the evening grog, he told us the strange news that Jamie Green,
the plum-cake *wallah*, had been discovered to be a spy from Lucknow, had been arrested, and was then undergoing examination at
the brigade-major's tent; and that it being too late to hang him
that night, he was to be made over to my guard for safe custody,
and that men had been warned for extra sentry on the guard-tent.
I need not say that I was very sorry to hear the information, for,
although a spy is at all times detested in the army, and no mercy is
ever shown to one, yet I had formed a strong regard for this man,
and a high opinion of his abilities in the short conversation I had
held with him the previous day; and during the interval I had been
thinking over how a man of his appearance and undoubted education could hold so low a position as that of a common camp-
follower. But now the news that he had been discovered to be a spy
accounted for the anomaly.

It would be needless for me to describe the bitter feeling of all
classes against the mutineers, or rebels, and for any one to be denounced as a spy simply added fuel to the flames of hatred. Asiatic
campaigns have always been conducted in a more remorseless
spirit than those between European nations, but the war of the
Mutiny, as I have before remarked in these reminiscences, was far
worse than the usual type of even Asiatic fighting. It was something horrible and down-right brutalising for an English army to
be engaged in such a struggle, in which no quarter was ever given
or asked. It was a war of downright butchery. Wherever the rebels
met a Christian or a white man he was killed without pity or remorse, and every native who had assisted any such to escape, or
was known to have concealed them, was as remorselessly put to
death wherever the rebels had the ascendant. And wherever a
European in power, either civil or military, met a rebel in arms, or
any native whatever on whom suspicion rested, his shrift was as
short and his fate as sure. The farce of putting an accused native on
his trial before any of the civil officers attached to the different
army-columns, after the civil power commenced to reassert its
authority, was simply a parody on justice and a protraction of
cruelty. Under martial law, punishment, whether deserved or not,
was stern but sharp. But the civilian officers attached to the
different movable columns for the trial of rebels, as far as they
came under my notice, were even more relentless. No doubt these
men excused themselves by the consideration that they were

engaged in suppressing rebellion and mutiny, and that the actors on the other side had perpetrated great crimes.* So far as the Commander-in-Chief was concerned, Sir Colin Campbell was utterly opposed to extreme measures, and deeply deplored the wholesale executions by the civil power. Although as a soldier he would have been the last man in the country to spare rebels caught with arms in their hands, or those whose guilt was well known. I well remember how emphatically I once heard him express his disgust when, on the march back from Fatehgarh to Cawnpore, he entered a mango-tope† full of rotting corpses, where one of those special commissioners had passed through with a movable column a few days before.

But I must return to my story. I had barely heard the news that Green had been arrested as a spy, when he was brought to my guard by some of the provost-marshal's staff, and handed over to me with instructions to keep him safe till he should be called for next morning. He was accompanied by the man who had carried his basket, who had also been denounced as one of the butchers at Cawnpore in July, 1857.

My prisoners had no sooner been made over to me, than several of the guard, as was usual in those days, proposed to bring some pork from the bazaar to break their castes, as a sort of preparation for their execution. This I at once denounced as a proceeding which I certainly would not tolerate so long as I held charge of the guard, and I warned the men that if anyone attempted to molest the prisoners, I should at once strip them of their belts, and place them in arrest for disobedience of orders and conduct unworthy of a British soldier, and the better-disposed portion of the guard at once applauded my resolution. I shall never forget the look of gratitude which came over the face of the unfortunate man who had called himself Jamie Green, when he heard me give these orders. He at once said it was an act of kindness which he had never expected, and for which he was truly grateful; and he un-hesitatingly pronounced his belief that Allah and his Prophet would

* It must also be remembered that these officials knew much more of the terrible facts attending the Mutiny—of the wholesale murder (and even worse) of English women and the slaughter of English children—than the rank and file were permitted to hear; and that they were also, both from their station and their experience, far better able to decide the measures best calculated to crush the imminent danger threatening our dominion in India.

† Mango-grove. [M.E.]

requite my kindness by bringing me safely through the remainder of the war. I thanked my prisoner for his good wishes and his prayers, and made him the only return in my power, viz., to cause his hands to be unfastened to allow him to perform his evening's devotions, and permitted him as much freedom as I possibly could, consistent with safe custody. His fellow-prisoner merely received my kindness with a scowl of sullen hatred, and when reproved by his master, I understood him to say he wished for no favour from infidel dogs; but he admitted that the sergeant *sahib* deserved a Muslim's gratitude for saving him from an application of pig's fat.

After allowing my prisoners to perform their evening devotions, and giving them such freedom as I could, I made up my mind to go without sleep that night, for it would have been a serious matter for me if either of these men had escaped. I also knew that by remaining on watch myself I could allow them more freedom, and I determined they should enjoy every privilege in my power for what would certainly be their last night on earth, since it was doubtful if they would be spared to see the sun rise. With this view, I sent for one of the Muhammadan shopkeepers from the regimental bazaar, and told him to prepare at my expense whatever food the prisoners would eat. To this the man replied that since I, a Christian, had shown so much kindness to a Muslim in distress, the Muhammadan shopkeepers in the bazaar would certainly be untrue to their faith if they should allow me to spend a single *pie* from my own pocket.

After being supplied with a savoury meal from the bazaar, followed by a fragrant hookah, to both of which he did ample justice, Jamie Green settled himself on a rug which had been lent to him, and said 'Thanks be to God', for having placed him under the charge of such a merciful *sahib* for this the last night of his life! 'Such', he continued, 'has been my *kismet*, and doubtless Allah will reward you, Sergeant *sahib*, in his own good time for your kindness to his oppressed and afflicted servant. You have asked me to give you some account of my life, and if it is really true that I am a spy. With regard to being a spy in the ordinary meaning of the term, I most emphatically deny the accusation. I am no spy; but I am an officer of the Begum's army, come out from Lucknow to gain reliable information of the strength of the army and siege-train being brought against us. I am the chief engineer of the army of Lucknow, and came out on a reconnoitring expedition, but Allah has not blessed my enterprise. I intended to have left on my return to Lucknow this evening, and if fate had been propitious, I would have reached it before sunrise tomorrow, for I had got all the information which was wanted; but I was tempted to visit Unao once more, being on the direct road to Lucknow, because I was anxious to see whether the siege-train and ammunition-park had commenced to move, and it was my misfortune to encounter that son of a defiled mother who denounced me as a spy. A contemptible wretch who, to save his own neck from the gallows (for he first sold the English), now wishes to divert attention from his former rascality by selling the lives of his own countrymen and co-religionists; but Allah is just, he will yet reap the reward of his treachery in the fires of Hell.*

'You ask me', continued the man, 'what my name is, and state that you intend to write an account of my misfortune to your friends in Scotland. Well, I have no objection. The people of England—and by England I mean Scotland as well—are just, and some of them may pity the fate of this servant of Allah. I have friends both in London and in Edinburgh, for I have twice visited both places. My name is Muhammad Ali Khan. I belong to one of the best families of Rohilkhand, and was educated in the Bareilly College, and took the senior place in all English subjects. From Bareilly College I passed to the Government Engineering College at Roorkee, and studied engineering for the Company's service, and passed out the senior student of my year, having gained many marks in excess of all the European pupils, both civil and military. But what was the result? I was nominated to the rank of *jemadar* of the Company's engineers, and sent to serve with a company on detached duty on the hill roads as a native commissioned officer, but actually subordinate to a European sergeant, a man who was my inferior in every way, except, perhaps, in mere brute strength, a man of little or no education, who would never have risen above the grade of a working-joiner in England. Like most ignorant men in authority, he exhibited all the faults of the Europeans which most irritate and disgust us, arrogance, insolence, and selfishness. Unless you learn the language of my countrymen, and mix with the better-educated people of this country, you will never

* This very man who denounced Jamie Green as a spy was actually hanged in Bareilly in the following May for having murdered his master in that station when the Mutiny first broke out.

understand nor estimate at its full extent the mischief which one such man does to your national reputation. One such example is enough to confirm all that your worst enemies can say about your national selfishness and arrogance, and makes the people treat your pretensions to liberality and sympathy as mere hypocrisy. I had not joined the Company's service from any desire for wealth, but from the hope of gaining honourable service; yet on the very threshold of that service I met with nothing but disgrace and dishonour, having to serve under a man whom I hated, yea, worse than hated, whom I despised. I wrote to my father, and requested his permission to resign, and he agreed with me that I, the descendant of princes, could not serve the Company under conditions such as I have described. I resigned the service and returned home, intending to offer my services to his late Majesty Nasir-ud-din, King of Oudh; but just when I reached Lucknow I was informed that his Highness Jang Bahadur of Nepal, who is now at Gorukhpur with an army of Gurkhas coming to assist in the loot of Lucknow, was about to visit England, and required a secretary well acquainted with the English language. I at once applied for the post, and being well backed by recommendations both from native princes and English officials, I secured the appointment, and in the suite of the Maharaja I landed in England for the first time, and, among other places, we visited Edinburgh, where your regiment, the Ninety-Third Highlanders, formed the guard of honour for the reception of his Highness. Little did I think when I saw a kilted regiment for the first time, that I should ever be a prisoner in their tents in the plains of Hindustan; but who can predict or avoid his fate?

'Well, I returned to India, and filled several posts at different native courts till 1854, when I was again asked to visit England in the suite of Azimullah Khan, whose name you must have often heard in connection with this mutiny and rebellion. On the death of the Peshwa, the Nana had appointed Azimullah Khan to be his agent. He, like myself, had received a good education in English, under Gunga Din, headmaster of the Government school at Cawnpore. Azimullah was confident that, if he could visit England, he would be able to have the decrees of Lord Dalhousie* against his master reversed, and when I joined him he was about to start for England, well supplied with money to engage the best lawyers,

* Governor-General of India 1848–56. [M.E.]

and also to bribe high officials, if necessary. But I need not give you any account of our mission. You already know that, so far as London drawing-rooms went, it proved a social success, but as far as gaining our end, a political failure; and we left England after spending over £50,000, to return to India *via* Constantinople in 1855. From Constantinople we visited the Crimea, where we witnessed the assault and defeat of the English on the 18th of June, and were much struck by the wretched state of both armies in front of Sebastopol. Thence we returned to Constantinople, and there met certain real or pretended Russian agents, who made large promises of material support if Azimullah could stir up a rebellion in India. It was then that I and Azimullah formed the resolution of attempting to overthrow the Company's Government, and, thank God, we have succeeded in doing that; for from the newspapers which you lent me, I see that the Company's rule has gone, and that their charter for robbery and confiscation will not be renewed. Although we have failed to wrest the country from the English, I hope we have done some good, and that our lives will not be sacrificed in vain; for I believe direct government under the English parliament will be more just than was that of the Company, and that there is yet a future before my oppressed and downtrodden countrymen, although I shall not live to see it.

'I do not speak, *sahib*, to flatter you or to gain your favour. I have already gained that, and I know that you cannot help me any farther than you are doing, and that if you could, your sense of duty would not let you. I know I must die; but the unexpected kindness which you have shown to me has caused me to speak my mind. I came to this tent with hatred in my heart, and curses on my lips; but your kindness to me, unfortunate, has made me, for the second time since I left Lucknow, ashamed of the atrocities committed during this rebellion. The first time was at Cawnpore a few days ago, when Colonel Napier of the Engineers was directing the blowing up of the Hindu temples on the Cawnpore *ghat*, and a deputation of Hindu priests came to him to beg that the temples might not be destroyed. "Now, listen to me," said Colonel Napier in reply to them; "you were all here when our women and children were murdered, and you also well know that we are not destroying these temples for vengeance, but for military considerations connected with the safety of the bridge of boats. But if any man among you can prove to me that he did a single act of kindness to any

Christian man, woman, or child, nay, if he can even prove that he uttered one word of intercession for the life of any one of them, I pledge myself to spare the temple where he worships." I was standing in the crowd close to Colonel Napier at the time, and I thought it was bravely spoken. There was no reply, and the cowardly Brahmins slunk away. Napier gave the signal and the temples leaped into the air; and I was so impressed with the justness of Napier's remarks that I too turned away, ashamed.'

On this I asked him, 'Were you in Cawnpore when the Mutiny broke out?' To which he replied: 'No, thank God! I was in my home in Rohilkhand; and my hands are unstained by the blood of anyone, excepting those who have fallen in the field of battle. I knew that the storm was about to burst, and had gone to place my wife and children in safety, and I was in my village when I heard the news of the mutinies at Meerut and Bareilly. I immediately hastened to join the Bareilly brigade, and marched with them for Delhi. There I was appointed engineer-in-chief, and set about strengthening the defences by the aid of a party of the Company's engineers which had mutinied on the march from Roorkee to Meerut. I remained in Delhi till it was taken by the English in September. I then made my way to Lucknow with as many men as I could collect of the scattered forces. We first marched to Muttra, where we were obliged to halt till I threw a bridge of boats across the Jumna for the retreat of the army. We had still a force of over thirty thousand men under the command of Prince Firoz Shah and General Bukht Khan. As soon as I reached Lucknow I was honoured with the post of chief-engineer. I was in Lucknow in November when your regiment assisted to relieve the Residency. I saw the horrible slaughter in the Secundrabagh. I had directed the defences of that place the night before, and was looking on from the Shah Najaf when you assaulted it. I had posted over three thousand of the best troops in Lucknow in the Secundrabagh, as it was the key to the position, and not a man escaped. I nearly fainted; my liver turned to water when I saw the green flag pulled down, and a Highland bonnet set up on the flagstaff which I had erected the night before. I knew then that all was over, and directed the guns of the Shah Najaf to open fire on the Secundrabagh. Since then I have planned and superintended the construction of all the defensive works in and around Lucknow. You will see them when you return, and if the sepoys and artillerymen stand firmly behind them, many of the

The Times correspondent looking on at the sacking of the Kaisarbagh

English army will lose the number of their mess, as you call it, before you again become masters of Lucknow.'

I then asked him if it was true that the man he had called Micky on our first acquaintance had been one of the men employed by the Nana to butcher the women and children at Cawnpore in July? To this he replied: 'I believe it is true, but I did not know this when I employed him; he was merely recommended to me as a man on whom I could depend. If I had known then that he was a murderer of women and children, I should have had nothing to do with him, for it is he who has brought bad luck on me; it is my *kismet*, and I must suffer. Your English proverb says, "You cannot touch pitch and escape defilement", and I must suffer; Allah is just. It is the conduct of wretches such as these that has brought the anger of Allah on our cause.' On this I asked him if he knew whether there was any truth in the report of the European women having been dishonoured before being murdered. '*Sahib*', he replied, 'you are a stranger to this country or you would not ask such a question. Any one who knows anything of the customs of this country and the strict rules of caste, knows that all such stories are lies, invented to stir up race-hatred, as if we had not enough of that on both sides already. That the women and children were cruelly murdered I admit, but not one of them was dishonoured; and all the sentences written on the walls of the houses in Cawnpore, such as, "We are at the mercy of savages, who have ravished young and old," and such like, which have appeared in the Indian papers and been copied from them into the English ones, are malicious forgeries, and were written on the walls after the reoccupation of Cawnpore by General Outram's and Havelock's forces. Although I was not there myself, I have spoken with many who were there, and I know that what I tell you is true.'

I then asked him if he could give me any idea of the reason that had led the Nana to order the commission of such a cold-blooded, cowardly crime. 'Asiatics', he said, 'are weak, and their promises are not to be relied on, but that springs more from indifference to obligations than from prearranged treachery. When they make promises, they intend to keep them; but when they find them inconvenient, they choose to forget them. And so it was, I believe, with the Nana Sahib. He intended to have spared the women and children, but they had an enemy in his *zenana* in the person of a female fiend who had formerly been a slave-girl, and there were many about the Nana (Azimullah Khan for one) who wished to see him so irretrievably implicated in rebellion that there would be no possibility for him to draw back. So this woman was powerfully supported in her evil counsel, and obtained permission to have the English ladies killed; and after the sepoys of the Sixth Native Infantry and the Nana's own guard had refused to do the horrible work, this woman went and procured the wretches who did it. This information I have from General Tantia Topi, who quarrelled with the Nana on this same matter. What I tell you is true: the murder of the European women and children at Cawnpore was a woman's crime, for there is no fiend equal to a female fiend; but what cause she had for enmity against the unfortunate ladies I don't know—I never inquired.'

I next asked Muhammad Ali Khan if he knew whether there was any truth in the stories about General Wheeler's daughter having shot four or five men with a revolver, and then leaped into the well at Cawnpore. 'All these stories', was his answer, 'are pure inventions with no foundation of truth. General Wheeler's daughter is still alive, and is now in Lucknow; she has become a Muslim, and has married according to Muhammadan law the man who protected her; whether she may ever return to her own people I know not.'

In such conversation I passed the night with my prisoner, and towards daybreak I permitted him to perform his ablutions and morning devotions, after which he once more thanked me, and prayed that Allah might reward me for my kindness to His oppressed servant. Once, and only once, did he show any weakness, in alluding to his wife and two boys in their far-away home in Rohilkhand, when he remarked that they would never know the fate of their unfortunate father. But he at once checked himself saying, 'I have read French history as well as English; I must remember Danton, and show no weakness.' He then produced a gold ring which was concealed among his hair, and asked me if I would accept it and keep it in remembrance of him, in token of his gratitude. It was, he said, the only thing he could give me, as everything of value had been taken from him when he was arrested. He went on to say that the ring in question was only a common one, not worth more than ten rupees, but that it had been given to him by a holy man in Constantinople as a talisman, though the charm had been broken when he had joined the unlucky man who was his fellow-prisoner. I accepted the ring, which he placed on my finger with a blessing and a prayer for my preservation, and he told me to look on it and remember Muhammad Khan when I was in front of the fortifications of Lucknow, and no evil would befall me. He had hardly finished speaking when a guard from the provost-marshal came with an order to take over the prisoners, and I handed this man over with a sincere feeling of pity for his fate.

Immediately after, I received orders that the division would march at sunrise for Lucknow, and that my party was to join the rear-guard, after the ammunition-park and siege-train had moved on. The sun was high in the heavens before we left the encamping-ground, and in passing under a tree on the side of the Cawnpore and Lucknow road, I looked up, and was horrified to see my late prisoner and his companion hanging stark and stiffened corpses! I could hardly repress a tear as I passed. But on the 11th of March, in the assault on the Begum Kothi, I remembered Muhammad Ali Khan and looked on the ring. I am thankful to say that I went through the rest of the campaign without a scratch, and the thoughts of my kindness to this unfortunate man certainly did not inspire me with any desire to shirk danger. I still have the ring, the only piece of Mutiny plunder I ever possessed and shall hand it down to my children together with the history of Muhammad Ali Khan.

11. SECOND ADVANCE ON LUCKNOW

AFTER leaving Unao, our division under Sir Edward Lugard reached Buntera, six miles from the Alambagh, on the 27th of February, and halted there till the 2nd of March, when we marched to the Dilkusha, encamping a short distance from the palace barely beyond reach of the enemy's guns, for they were able at times to throw round-shot into our camp. We then settled down for the siege and capture of Lucknow; but the work before us was considered tame and unimportant when compared with that of the relief of the previous November. Every soldier in the camp clearly recognised that the capture of the doomed city was simply a matter of time—a few days more or less—and the task before us a mere matter of routine, nothing to be compared to the exciting exertions which we had to put forth for the relief of our countrywomen and their children.

At the time of the annexation of Oudh Lucknow was estimated to contain from eight to nine hundred thousand inhabitants, or as many as Delhi and Benares put together. The camp and bazaars of our force were full of reports of the great strength and determination of the enemy, and certainly all the chiefs of Oudh, Muhammadan and Hindu, had joined the standard of the Begum and had sworn to fight for their young king Birjis Qadr. All Oudh was therefore still against us, and we held only the ground covered by the British guns. Bazaar reports estimated the enemy's strength at from two hundred and fifty to three hundred thousand fighting men, with five hundred guns in position; but in the Commander-in-Chief's camp the strength of the enemy was computed at sixty thousand regulars, mutineers who had lately served the Company, and about seventy thousand irregulars, matchlock-men, armed police, dacoits, etc., making a total of one hundred and thirty thousand fighting men. To fight this large army, sheltered behind entrenchments and loopholed walls, the British force, even after being joined by Jang Bahadur's Gurkhas,* mustered only about thirty-one thousand men of all arms, and one hundred and sixty-four guns.

See Introduction, p. 8. [M.E.]

From the heights of the Dilkusha in the cool of the early morning, Lucknow, with its numerous domed mosques, minarets, and
palaces, looked very picturesque. I don't think I ever saw a prettier
scene than that presented on the morning of the 3rd of March,
1858, when the sun rose, and Captain Peel and his Blue-jackets
were getting their heavy guns, 68-pounders, into position. From
the Dilkusha, even without the aid of telescopes, we could see that
the defences had been greatly strengthened, since we retired from
Lucknow in November, and I called to mind the warning of Jamie
Green, that if the enemy stood to their guns like men behind those
extensive earthworks, many of the British force would lose the
number of their mess before we could take the city; and although
the Indian papers which reached our camp affected to sneer at the
Begum, Hazrat Mahal, and the legitimacy of her son Birjis
Qadr, whom the mutineers had proclaimed King of Oudh, they
had evidently the support of the whole country, for every chief and
*zemindar** of any importance had joined them.

On the morning after we had pitched our camp in the Dilkusha
park, I went out with Sergeant Peter Gillespie, our deputy provost-
marshal, to take a look round the bazaars, and just as we turned a
corner on our way back to camp, we met some gentlemen in
civilian dress, one of whom turned out to be Mr Russell,† *The
Times'* correspondent, whom we never expected to have seen in
India. 'Save us, sir!' said Peter Gillespie. 'Is that you, Maister
Russell? I never did think of meeting you here, but I am right glad
to see you, and so will all our boys be!' After a short chat and a
few inquiries about the regiment, Mr Russell asked when we
expected to be in Lucknow, to which Peter Gillespie replied:
'Well, I dinna ken, sir, but when Sir Colin likes to give the order,
we'll just advance and take it.'

On the 4th of March the Ninety-Third, a squadron of the Ninth
Lancers, and a battery of artillery, were marched to the banks of
the Gumti opposite Bibipur House, to form a guard for the engineers engaged in throwing a pontoon bridge across the Gumti. The
weather was now very hot in the day-time, and as we were well
beyond the range of the enemy's guns, we were allowed to undress
by companies and bathe in the river. As far as I can remember, we
were two days on this duty. During the forenoon of the second day

* Landowner. [M.E.]
† William Howard Russell, the first 'War Correspondent'. [M.E.]

the Commander-in-Chief visited us, and the regiment fell in to receive him, because, he said, he had something of importance to communicate. When formed up, Sir Colin told us that he had just received despatches from home, and among them a letter from the Queen in which the Ninety-Third was specially mentioned. He then pulled the letter out of his pocket, and read the paragraph alluded to, which ran as follows, as nearly as I remembered to note it down after it was read: 'The Queen wishes Sir Colin to convey the expression of her great admiration and gratitude to all European as well as native troops who have fought so nobly and so gallantly for the relief of Lucknow, amongst whom the Queen is rejoiced to see the Ninety-Third Highlanders.' Colonel Leith-Hay at once called for three cheers for her Majesty the Queen, which were given with hearty good-will, followed by three more for the Commander-in-Chief. The colonel then requested Sir Colin to return the thanks of the officers, non-commissioned officers, and men of the regiment to her Majesty the Queen for her most gracious message, and for her special mention of the Ninety-Third, an honour which no one serving in the regiment would ever forget. To this Sir Colin replied that nothing would give him greater pleasure than to comply with this request; but he had still more news to communicate. He had also a letter from his Royal Highness the Duke of Cambridge to read to us, which he proceeded to do as follows: 'One line in addition to my letter addressed to you this morning, to say that, in consequence of the colonelcy of the Ninety-Third Highlanders having become vacant by the death of General Parkinson, I have recommended the Queen to remove you to the command of that distinguished and gallant corps, with which you have been so much associated, not alone at the present moment in India, but also during the whole of the campaign in the Crimea. I thought such an arrangement would be agreeable to yourself, and I know that it is the highest compliment that her Majesty could pay to the Ninety-Third Highlanders to see their dear old chief at their head.' As soon as Sir Colin had read this letter, the whole regiment cheered till we were hoarse; and when Sir Colin's voice could again be heard, he called for the master-tailor to go to the headquarters' camp to take his measure to send home for a uniform of the regiment for him, feather bonnet and all complete.

Early on the 7th of March General Outram's division crossed the Gumti by the bridge of boats, and we returned to our tents at the Dilkusha. About midday we could see Outram's division, of which the Seventy-Ninth Cameron Highlanders formed one of the infantry corps, driving the enemy before them in beautiful style. We saw also the Queen's Bays, in their bright scarlet uniform and brass helmets, make a splendid charge, scattering the enemy like sheep. In this charge Major Percy Smith and several men galloped right through the enemy's lines, and were surrounded and killed. Spies reported that Major Smith's head was cut off, and, with his helmet, plume, and uniform, paraded through the streets of Lucknow as the head of the Commander-in-Chief. But the triumph of the enemy was short. On the 8th General Outram was firmly established on the north bank of the Gumti, with a siege-train of twenty-two heavy guns, with which he completely turned and enfiladed the enemy's strong position.

On the 9th of March we were ordered to take our dinners at twelve o'clock, and shortly after that hour our division, consisting of the Thirty-Eighth, Forty-Second, Fifty-Third, Ninetieth, Ninety-Third, and Fourth Punjab Infantry, was under arms, screened by the Dilkusha palace and the garden walls round it, and Peel's Blue-jackets were pouring shot and shell, with now and again a rocket, into the Martinière as fast as ever they could load. About two o'clock the order was given for the advance—the Forty-Second to lead and the Ninety-Third to support; but we no sooner emerged from the shelter of the palace and garden-walls than the orderly advance became a rushing torrent. Both regiments dashed down the slope abreast, and the earthworks, trenches, and rifle-pits in front of the Martinière were cleared, the enemy flying before us as fast as their legs could carry them. We pursued them right through the gardens, capturing their first line of works along the canal in front of Banks's bungalow and the Begum's palace [Begum Kothi].

There we halted for the night, our heavy guns and mortar-batteries being advanced from the Dilkusha; and I, with some men from my company, was sent on piquet to a line of unroofed huts in front of one of our mortar-batteries, for fear the enemy from the Begum's palace might make a rush on the mortars. This piquet was not relieved till the morning of the 11th, when I learned that my company had been sent back as camp-guards, the captains of companies having drawn lots for this service, as all were equally anxious to take part in the assault on the Begum's palace, and it

was known the Ninety-Third were to form the storming-party.
As soon as the works should be breached, I and the men who were
with me on the advance-piquet were to be sent to join Captain
M'Donald's company, instead of going back to our own in camp.
After being relieved from piquet, our little party set about preparing some food. Our own company having gone back to camp,
no rations had been drawn for us, and our haversacks were almost
empty; so I will here relate a mild case of cannibalism. Of the men
of my own company who were with me on this piquet one was
Andrew M'Onvill—Handy Andy, as he was called in the regiment
—a good-hearted, jolly fellow, and as full of fun and practical jokes
as his namesake,* Lever's hero—a thorough Paddy from Armagh,
a soldier as true as the steel of a Damascus blade or a Scotch
Andrea Ferrara. Others were Sandy Proctor, soldier-servant to
Dr Munro, and George Patterson, the son of the carrier of Ballater
in Aberdeenshire. We were joined by John M'Leod, the pipe-
major, and one or two more. We got into an empty hut, well
sheltered from the bullets of the enemy, and Handy Andy sallied
out on a foraging expedition for something in the way of food. He
had a friend in the Fifty-Third who was connected in some way
with the quartermaster's department, and always well supplied
with extra provender. The Fifty-Third were on our right, and
there Handy Andy found his friend, and returned with a good big
steak, cut from an artillery gun-bullock which had been killed by a
round-shot; also some sheep's liver and a haversack full of biscuits,
with plenty of pumpkin to make a good stew. There was no lack
of cooking-pots in the huts around, and plenty of wood for fuel, so
we kindled a fire, and very soon had an excellent stew in preparation. But the enemy pitched some shells into our position, and one
burst close to a man named Tim Drury, a big stout fellow, killing
him on the spot. I forgot which company he belonged to, but his
body lay where he fell, just outside our hut, with one thigh nearly
torn away.

My readers must not for a moment think that such a picture in
the foreground took away our appetites in the least. There is
nothing like a campaign for making one callous and selfish, and
developing the qualities of the wild beast in one's nature; and the
thought which rises uppermost is—well, it is his turn now, and it

* Character in a novel by the Victorian author, Charles James Lever (1806–72).
[M.E.]

may be mine next, and there is no use in being downhearted! Our steak had been broiled to a turn, and our stew almost cooked, when we noticed tiffin and breakfast combined arrive for the European officers of the Fourth Punjab Regiment and some others who were waiting sheltered by the walls of a roofless hut near where we were. Among them was a young fellow, Lieutenant Fitzgerald Cologan, attached to some native regiment, a great favourite with the Ninety-Third for his pluck. John M'Leod at once proposed that Handy Andy should go and offer him half of our broiled steak, and ask him for a couple of bottles of beer for our dinner, as it might be the last time we should have the chance of drinking his health. He and the other officers with him accepted the steak with thanks, and Andy returned, to our no small joy, with two quart bottles of Bass's beer. But, unfortunately he had attracted the attention of Charley F., the greatest glutton in the Ninety-Third, who was so well known for his greediness that no one would chum with him. Charley was a long-legged, humpbacked, cadaverous-faced, bald-headed fellow, who had joined the regiment as a volunteer from the Seventy-Second before we left Dover in the spring of 1857, and on account of his long legs and humpback, combined with the inordinate capacity of his stomach and an incurable habit of grumbling, he had been rechristened the 'Camel', before we had proceeded many marches with that useful animal in India.

Our mutual congratulations were barely over on the aquisition of the two bottles of beer, when, to our consternation, we saw the Camel dodging from cover to cover, as the enemy were keeping up a heavy fire on our position, and if anyone exposed himself in the least, a shower of bullets was sent whistling round him. However, the Camel, with a due regard to the wholeness of his skin, steadily made way towards our hut. We all knew that if he were admitted to a share of our stew, very little would be left for ourselves. John M'Leod and I suggested that we should, at the risk of quarrelling with him, refuse to allow him any share, but Handy Andy said, 'Leave him to me, and if a bullet doesn't knock him over as he comes round the next corner, I'll put him off asking for a share of the stew.' By that time we had finished our beer. Well, the Camel took good care to dodge the bullets of Jack Pandy, and he no sooner reached a sheltered place in front of the hut, than Andy called out: 'Come along, Charley, you are just in time; we got a slice of a nice steak from an artillery-bullock this morning, and because it was too small alone for a dinner for the four of us, we have just stewed it with a slice from Tim Drury, and bedad it's first-rate! Tim tastes for all the world like fresh pork'; and with that Andy picked out a piece of sheep's liver on the prongs of his fork, and offered it to Charley as part of Tim Drury, at the same time requesting him not to mention the circumstance to anyone. This was too much for the Camel's stomach. He plainly believed Andy, and turned away, as if he would be sick. However, he recovered himself, and replied: 'No, thank you; hungry as I am, it shall never be in the power of anyone to tell my auld mither in the Grass Market o' Edinboro' that her Charley had become a cannibal! But if you can spare me a drop of the beer I'll be thankful for it, for the sight of your stew has made me feel unco' queer.' We expressed our sorrow that the beer was all drunk before we had seen Charley performing his oblique advance, and Andy again pressed him to partake of a little of the stew; but Charley refused to join, and sitting down in a sheltered spot in the corner of our roofless mud-hut, made wry faces at the relish evinced by the rest of us over our savoury stew. The Camel eventually discovered that he had been made a fool of, and he never forgave us for cheating him out of a share of the savoury mess.

12. FINAL RELIEF OF LUCKNOW

WE had barely finished our meal when we noticed a stir among the staff-officers, and a consultation taking place between General Sir Edward Lugard, Brigadier Adrian Hope, and Colonel Napier. Suddenly the order was given to the Ninety-Third to fall in. This was quietly done, the officers taking their places, the men tightening their belts and pressing their bonnets firmly on their heads, loosening the ammunition in their pouches, and seeing that the springs of their bayonets held tight. Thus we stood for a few seconds, when Brigadier Hope passed the signal for the assault on the Begum Kothi. Just before the signal was given two men from the Fifty-Third rushed up to us with a soda-water bottle full of grog. One of them was Lance-Corporal Robert Clary the other was the friend of Andrew M'Onvill, who had supplied us with the steaks for our 'cannibal feast'. I may mention that Lance-Corporal Clary was the same man who led the party of the Fifty-Third to capture the guns at the Kali Nadi bridge, and who called out: 'Three cheers for the Commander-in-Chief, boys,' when Sir Colin Campbell was threatening to send the regiment to the rear for breach of orders. Clary was a County Limerick boy of the right sort, such as filled the ranks of our Irish regiments. No Fenian nor Home Ruler; but ever ready to uphold the honour of the British Army by land or by sea, and to share the contents of his haversack or his glass of grog with a comrade; one of those whom Scott immortalises in *The Vision of Don Roderick*.

> Hark! from yon stately ranks what laughter rings,
>   Mingling wild mirth with war's stern minstrelsy,
> His jest while each blithe comrade round him flings,
>   And moves to death with military glee!
> Boast, Erin, boast them! tameless, frank, and free,
>   In kindness warm, and fierce in danger known,
> Rough Nature's children, humorous as she.

When Captain M'Donald, whose company we had joined, saw the two Fifty-Third boys, he told them that they had better rejoin their own regiment. Clary replied, 'Sure, Captain, you don't mean

it;' and seeing Dr Munro, our surgeon, busy giving directions to
his assistants and arranging bandages, etc., in a *dooly*, Clary went
on: 'We have been sent by Lieutenant Munro of our company to
take care of his namesake your doctor, who never thinks of himself,
but is sure to be in the thick of the fight, looking out for wounded
men. You of the Ninety-Third don't appreciate his worth. There's
not another doctor in the army to equal him or to replace him
should he get knocked over in this scrimmage, and we of the Fifty-
Third have come to take care of him.' 'If that is the case,' said
Captain M'Donald, 'I'll allow you to remain; but you must take
care that no harm befalls our doctor, for he is a great friend of
mine.' And with that Captain M'Donald stepped aside and plucked
a rose from a bush close by (we were then formed up in what had
been a beautiful garden), and going up to Munro he gave him the
flower saying, 'Good-bye, old friend, keep this for my sake.' I have
often recalled this incident and wondered if poor Captain M'Donald
had any presentiment that he would be killed! Although he had
been a captain for some years, he was still almost a boy. He was a
son of General Sir John M'Donald, K.C.B., of Dalchosnie, Perth-
shire, and was wounded in his right arm early in the day by a
splinter from a shell, but he refused to go to the rear, and remained
at the head of his company, led it through the breach, and was shot
down just inside, two bullets striking him almost at once, one right
in his throat just over the breast-bone, as he was waving his claymore and cheering on his company. After the fight was over I made
my way to where the dead were collected and cut off a lock of his
hair and sent it to a young lady, Miss M. E. Ainsworth, of In-
verighty House, Forfar, who, I knew, was acquainted with Captain
M'Donald's family. I intended the lock of hair for his mother, and
I did not know if his brother officers would think of sending any
memento of him. I don't know if ever the lock of hair reached his
mother or not. When I went to do this I found Captain M'Donald's
soldier-servant crying beside the lifeless body of his late master,
wringing his hands and saying, 'Oh! but it was a shame to kill him.'
And so it was! I never saw a more girlish-looking face than his was
in death; his features were so regular, and looked strangely like
those of a wax doll, which was, I think, partly the effect of the
wound in the throat. But to return to the assault.

When Captain M'Donald fell, the company was led by the
senior lieutenant, and about twenty yards inside the breach in the

outer rampart we were stopped by a ditch nearly eighteen feet
wide and at least twelve to fourteen feet deep. It was easy enough
to slide down to the bottom; the difficulty was to get up on the
other side! However, there was no hesitation; the stormers dashed
into the ditch, and running along to the right in search of some
place where we could get up on the inside, we met part of the
grenadier company headed by Lieutenant E. S. Wood, an active
and daring young officer. I may here mention that there were two
lieutenants of the name of Wood at this time in the Ninety-Third.
One belonged to my company; his name was S. E. Wood and he
was severely wounded at the relief of Lucknow and was, at the time
of which I am writing, absent from the regiment. The one to whom
I now refer was Lieutenant E. S. Wood of the grenadier company.
When the two parties in the ditch met, both in search of a place to
get out, Mr Wood got on the shoulders of another grenadier and
somehow scrambled up, claymore in hand. He was certainly the first
man inside the inner works of the Begum's palace, and when the
enemy saw him emerge from the ditch they fled to barricade doors
and windows to prevent us getting into the buildings. His action
saved us, for the whole of us might have been shot like rats in the
ditch if they had attacked Mr Wood, instead of flying when they
saw the tall grenadier claymore in hand. As soon as he saw the
coast clear the lieutenant lay down on the top of the ditch, and was
thus able to reach down and catch hold of the men's rifles by the
bends of the bayonets; and with the aid of the men below pushing
up behind, we were all soon pulled out of the ditch. When all were
up, one of the men turned to Mr Wood and said: 'If any officer
in the regiment deserves to get the Victoria Cross, sir, you do; for
besides the risk you have run from the bullets of the enemy, it's
more than a miracle that you're not shot by our own rifles; they're
all on full-cock.' And so it was! Seizing loaded rifles on full-cock
by the muzzles, and pulling more than a score of men out of a deep
ditch, was a dangerous thing to do; but no one thought of the
danger, nor did anyone think of even easing the spring to half-
cock, much less of firing his rifle off before being pulled up. However, Mr Wood escaped.

By the time we got out of the ditch we found every door and
window of the palace buildings barricaded, and every loop-hole
defenced by an invisible enemy. But one barrier after another was
forced, and men in small parties, headed by the officers, got

possession of the inner square, where the enemy in large numbers
stood ready for the struggle. But no thought of unequal numbers
held us back. The command was given: 'Keep well together, men,
and use the bayonet; give them the Secundrabagh and the sixteenth
of November over again.' I need not describe the fight. It raged
for about two hours from court to court, and from room to room;
the pipe-major, John M'Leod, playing the pipes inside as calmly as
if he had been walking round the officers mess-tent at a regimental
festival. When all was over, General Sir Edward Lugard, who
commanded the division, complimented the pipe-major on his
coolness and bravery: 'Ah, sir,' said John, 'I knew our boys would
fight all the better when cheered by the bagpipes.'

Within about two hours from the time the signal for the assault
was given, over eight hundred and sixty of the enemy lay dead
within the inner court, and no quarter was sought or given. By
this time we were broken up in small parties in a series of separate
fights, all over the different detached buildings of the palace. Captain M'Donald being dead, the men who had been on piquet with
me joined a party under Lieutenant Sergison, and while breaking
in the door of a room, Mr Sergison was shot dead at my side with
several men. When we had partly broken in the door, I saw that
there was a large number of the enemy inside the room, well armed
with swords and spears, in addition to fire-arms of all sorts, and,
not wishing to be either killed myself or have more of the men who
were with me killed, I divided my party, placing some at each side
of the door to shoot every man who showed himself, or attempted
to rush out. I then sent two men back to the breach, where I knew
Colonel Napier with his engineers were to be found, to get a few
bags of gunpowder with slow-matches fixed, to light and pitch into
the room. Instead of finding Napier, the two men sent by me found
the redoubtable Major Hodson who had accompanied Napier as a
volunteer in the storming of the palace. Hodson did not wait for
the powder-bags, but, after showing the men where to go for them,
came running up himself, sabre in hand. 'Where are the rebels?' he
said. I pointed to the door of the room, and Hodson, shouting
'Come on!' was about to rush in. I implored him not to do so,
saying, 'It's certain death; wait for the powder; I've sent men for
powder-bags.' Hodson made a step forward, and I put out my
hand to seize him by the shoulder to pull him out of the line of the
doorway, when he fell back shot through the chest. He gasped out

a few words, either 'Oh, my wife!' or, 'Oh, my mother!'—I cannot rightly remember—but was immediately choked by blood. I assisted to get him lifted into a *dooly* (by that time the bearers had got in and were collecting the wounded who were unable to walk), and I sent him back to where the surgeons were, fully expecting that he would be dead before anything could be done for him. It will thus be seen that the assertion that Major Hodson was looting when he was killed is untrue.* No looting had been commenced, not even by Jang Bahadur's Gurkhas. That Major Hodson was killed through his own rashness cannot be denied; but for anyone to say that he was looting is a cruel slander on one of the bravest of Englishmen.

Shortly after I had lifted poor Hodson into the *dooly* and sent him away in charge of his orderly, the two men who had gone for the powder came up with several bags, with slow-matches fixed in them. These we ignited, and then pitched the bags in through the door. Two or three bags very soon brought the enemy out, and they were bayoneted down without mercy. One of the men who were with me was Mr Rule, a powerful young man of the light company. Rule rushed in among the rebels, using both bayonet and butt of his rifle, shouting, 'Revenge for the death of Hodson!' and he killed more than half the men single-handed. By this time we had been over two hours inside the breach, and almost all opposition had ceased. Lieutenant and Adjutant 'Willie' MacBean, as he was known to the officers, and 'Paddy' MacBean to the men, encountered a *havildar*,† a *naik*‡ and nine sepoys at one gate, and killed the whole eleven, one after the other. The *havildar* was the last; and by the time he got out through the narrow gate, several men came to the assistance of MacBean, but he called to them not to interfere, and the *havildar* and he went at it with their swords. At length MacBean made a feint cut, but instead gave the point, and put his sword through the chest of his opponent. For this MacBean got the Victoria Cross, mainly, I believe, because Sir Edward Lugard, the general in command of the division, was looking down from the ramparts above and saw the whole affair. I don't think that MacBean himself thought he had done anything extraordinary. He was an Inverness-shire ploughman before he enlisted.§ There were still a number of old soldiers in the regiment who had been privates with MacBean when I enlisted, and many anecdotes were

---

* See Introduction, p. 11. [M.E.]
† Native sergeant. [M.E.]
‡ Native corporal. [M.E.]
§ He died a major-general. [M.E.]

related about him. One of these was that when MacBean first
joined, he walked with a rolling gait, and the drill-corporal was
rather abusive with him when learning his drill. At last he became
so offensive that another recruit proposed to MacBean, who was a
very powerful man, that they should call the corporal behind the
canteen in the barrack-yard and give him a good thrashing, to
which proposal MacBean replied: 'Toots, toots, man, that would
never do. I am going to command this regiment before I leave it,*
and it would be an ill beginning to be brought before the colonel
for thrashing the drill-corporal!' I have seen it stated that he was a
drummer-boy in the regiment, but that is not correct. He was kept
seven years lance-corporal, partly because promotion went slow
in the Ninety-Third, but several were promoted over him because,
at the time of the disruption in the Church of Scotland, MacBean
joined the Free Kirk party. The Ninety-Third was constituted as
much after the arrangements of a Highland parish as those of a
regiment in the army; and, to use the words of old Colonel Sparks
who commanded, MacBean was passed over four promotions
because 'He was a d—d Free Kirker'.

But I must hark back to my story and to the Begum Kothi on
the evening of the 11th of March, 1858. By the time darkness set in
all opposition had ceased, but there were still numbers of the
mutineers hiding in the rooms. Our loss was small compared with
that inflicted on the enemy. Our regiment had one captain, one
lieutenant, and thirteen rank and file killed; Lieutenant Grimston,
Ensign Hastie, and forty-five men wounded. Many of the wounded
died afterwards; but eight hundred and sixty of the enemy lay dead
in the centre court alone, and many hundreds more were killed in
the different enclosures and buildings. That night we bivouacked
in the courts of the palace, placing strong guards all round. When
daylight broke on the morning of the 12th of March, the sights
around were horrible. I have already mentioned that many sepoys
had to be dislodged from the close rooms around the palace by
exploding bags of gunpowder among them, and this set fire to their
clothing and to whatever furniture there was in the rooms; and
when day broke on the 12th, there were hundreds of bodies all
round, some still burning and others half-burnt, and the stench was
sickening. However, the Begum's palace was the key to the
enemy's position. During the day large parties of camp-followers

* He did. [M.E.]

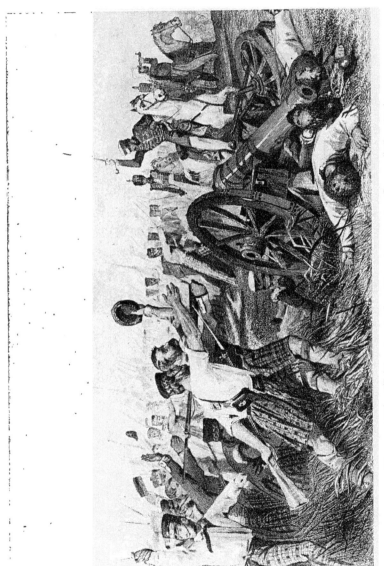

Charge of the Highlanders before Cawnpore, under General Havelock

were brought in to drag out the dead of the enemy, and throw them into the ditch which had given us so much trouble to cross, and our batteries were advanced to bombard the Imambara and Kaisarbagh.

During the forenoon of the 12th, I remember seeing Mr Russell of *The Times* going round making notes, and General Lugard telling him to take care and not to attempt to go into any dark room for fear of being 'potted' by concealed Pandies. Many such were hunted out during the day, and as there was no quarter for them they fought desperately. We had one sergeant killed at this work and several men wounded. During the afternoon a divisional order by General Sir Edward Lugard was read to us, as follows:

'Major-General Sir Edward Lugard begs to thank Brigadier the Honourable Adrian Hope, Colonel Leith-Hay, and the officers and men of the Ninety-Third who exclusively carried the position known as the Begum Kothi. No words are sufficient to express the gallantry, devotion, and fearless intrepidity displayed by every officer and man in the regiment. The Major-General will not fail to bring their conduct prominently to the notice of his Excellency the Commander-in-Chief.'

During the day Sir Colin himself visited the position, and told us that arrangements would be made for our relief the following day, and on Saturday the 13th we returned to camp and rested all the following Sunday. So far as I remember, the two men of the Fifty-Third, Lance-Corporal Clary and his comrade, remained with us till after the place was taken, and then returned to their own regiment when the fighting was over, reporting to Lieutenant Munro that they had gone to take care of his brother, Doctor Munro of the Ninety-Third.

There were many individual acts of bravery performed during the assault, and it is difficult to single them out. But before closing this chapter I may relate a rather laughable incident that happened to a man of my company named Johnny Ross. He was a little fellow, and there were two of the same name in the company, one tall and the other short, so they were named respectively John and Johnny. Before falling in for the assault on the Begum's palace, Johnny Ross and George Puller, with some others, had been playing cards in a sheltered corner, and in some way quarrelled over the game. When the signal was given for the 'fall in', Puller and Ross were still arguing the point in dispute, and Puller told Ross to 'shut up'. Just at that very moment a spent bullet struck Ross in the mouth, knocking in four of his front teeth. Johnny thought it was Puller who had struck him, and at once returned the blow; when Puller quietly replied, 'You d——d fool, it was not I who struck you; you've got a bullet in your mouth.' And so it was: Johnny Ross put up his hand to his mouth, and spat out four front teeth and a leaden bullet. He at once apologised to Puller for having struck him, and added, 'How will I manage to bite my cartridges the noo?'

We returned to our tents at the Dilkusha on Saturday, the 13th, and the whole regiment formed a funeral party for our killed near the palace.

13. THE AFTERMATH OF VICTORY

ON the return of the regiment to camp at the Dilkusha on the 13th of March I was glad to get back to my own company. The men were mortified because they had not shared in the honour of the assault on the Begum's palace; but as some compensation the company had formed the guard-of-honour for the reception of the Maharaja Jang Bahadur, Commander-in-Chief of the Nepalese Army, who had just reached Lucknow and had been received in state by Sir Colin Campbell on the afternoon of the 11th, at the moment when the regiment was engaged in the assault on the palace. The meeting had at first proved a rather stiff ceremonial affair, but Jang Bahadur and his officers had hardly been presented and taken their seats, when a commotion was heard outside, and Captain Hope Johnstone, aide-de-camp to General Sir William Mansfield, covered with powder-smoke and the dust of battle, strode up the centre of the guard-of-honour with a message to the Commander-in-Chief from Mansfield, informing him that the Ninety-Third had taken the Begum's palace, the key of the enemy's position, with slight loss to themselves, but that they had killed over a thousand of the enemy. This announcement put an end to all ceremony on the part of Sir Colin, who jumped to his feet, rubbing his hands, and calling out, 'I knew they would do it! I knew my boys of the Ninety-Third would do it!' Then telling Captain Metcalfe to interpret the news to the Maharaja, and pointing to the guard-of-honour, Sir Colin said: 'Tell him that these men are part of the regiment that has done this daring feat. Tell him also that they are *my* regiment; I'm their colonel!' The Maharaja looked pleased, and replied that he remembered having seen the regiment when he visited England in 1852. As I have already said, the Ninety-Third had formed a guard-of-honour for him when in Edinburgh, and there were still many men in the regiment who remembered seeing Jang Bahadur. There was an oft-repeated story among the old soldiers that the Maharaja was so pleased at the sight of them that he had proposed to buy the whole regiment, and was somewhat surprised to learn that British soldiers were volunteers and could not be sold, even to gratify the Maharaja of Nepal.

After returning to camp on the 13th of March, the regiment was allowed to rest till the 17th, but returned to the city on the morning of the 18th, taking up a position near the Imambara and the Kaisar-bagh, both of which had been captured when we were in camp. We relieved the Forty-Second, and the sights that then met our eyes in the streets of Lucknow defy description. The city was in the hands of plunderers; Europeans and Sikhs, Gurkhas, and camp-followers of every class, aided by the scum of the native population. Every man in fact was doing what was right in his own eyes, and 'Hell broke loose' is the only phrase in the English language that can give one who has never seen such a sight any idea of the scenes in and around the Imambara, the Kaisarbagh, and adjacent streets. The Sikhs and Gurkhas were by far the most proficient plunderers, because they instinctively knew where to look for the most valuable loot. The European soldiers did not understand the business, and articles that might have proved a fortune to many were readily parted with for a few rupees in cash and a bottle of grog. But the gratuitous destruction of valuable property that could not be carried off was appalling. Colour-Sergeant Graham, of Captain Burroughs' company, rescued from the fire a bundle of Govern-ment-of-India promissory notes to the value of over a *lakh* of rupees, and Mr Kavanagh, afterwards discovering the rightful owner, secured for Sergeant Graham a reward of five per cent on the amount. But with few exceptions the men of the Ninety-Third got very little. I could fill a volume on the plunder of Lucknow, and the sights which are still vividly impressed on my memory.

Before I proceed to other subjects, and to make my recollections as instructive as possible for young soldiers, I may mention some serious accidents that happened through the explosions of gun-powder left behind by the enemy. One most appalling accident occurred in the house of a nobleman named Ashraf-ud-danla, in which a large quantity of gunpowder had been left; this was accidentally exploded, killing two officers and forty men of the Engineers, and a great number of camp-followers, of whom no account was taken. The poor men who were not killed outright were so horribly scorched that they all died in the greatest agony within a few hours of the accident, and for days explosions with more or less loss of life occurred all over the city. From the deplorable accidents that happened, which reasonable care might have prevented, I could enumerate the loss of over a hundred men.

By the accident in the house of Ashraf ud-danla, two of our most distinguished and promising Engineer officers—Captains Brownlow and Clarke—lost their lives, with forty of the most valuable branch of the service. All through the Mutiny I never forgot my own experience in the Shah Najaf; and wherever I could prevent it, I never allowed men to go into unexplored rooms with lighted pipes, or to force open locked doors by the usual method of firing a loaded rifle into the lock. After the assault on a city like Lucknow some license and plundering is inevitable, and where discipline is relaxed accidents are sure to happen; but a judicious use of the provost-marshal's cat would soon restore discipline and order. Whatever opponents of the lash may say, my own firm opinion is that the provost-marshal's cat is the only general to restore order in times like those I am describing. I would have no courts-martial, drum-head or otherwise; but simply give the provost-marshal a strong guard of picked men and several sets of triangles, with full power to tie up every man, no matter what his rank, caught plundering, and give him from one to four dozen, not across the shoulders, but across the breech, as judicial floggings are administered in our jails; and if these were combined with roll-calls at short intervals, plundering, which is a most dangerous pastime, would soon be put down. In time of war soldiers ought to be taught to treat every house or room of an assaulted position as a powder-magazine until explored. I am surprised that cautions on this head have been so long overlooked.

As before stated, the Ninety-Third did not get much plunder, but in expelling the enemy from some mosques and other strong buildings near the Imambara on the 21st of March, one company came across the tomb-model or royal *tazia*, and the Muharram paraphernalia which had been made at enormous expense for the celebration of the last Muharram in Lucknow in 1857.

I learned from native troopers that the golden *tazia* belonging to the crown jewels of Lucknow having accompanied the king to Calcutta,* a new one was made, for which the Muhammadan population of Lucknow subscribed *lakhs* of rupees. I was told by a native jeweller, who was in Lucknow in 1857, that the crescent and star alone of the new *tazia* made for the young 'king', Birjis Qadr, cost five *lakhs* of rupees. Be that as it may, it fell to a company of the Ninety-Third to assault the Durgah [shrine], where all this

* Wajid Ali Shah, last king of Oudh, was deposed in February, 1856, and retired to Calcutta. [M.E.]

consecrated paraphernalia was stored, and there they found this
golden *tazia*, with all the gold-embroidered standards, saddle, and
saddle-cloth, the gold quiver and arrows of Duldul.* There was at
the time I write, a certain lieutenant in the company whom I shall
call Jamie Blank. He was known to be very poor, and it was reported in the regiment that he used regularly to remit half of his
lieutenant's pay to support a widowed mother and a sister, and this
fact made the men of the company consider Jamie Blank entitled
to a share in the loot. So when the *tazia* was discovered, not being
very sure whether the diamonds in the crescent and star on the
dome were real or imitation, they settled to cut off the whole dome,
and give it to Jamie; which they did. I don't know where Jamie
Blank disposed of this particular piece of loot, but I was informed
that it eventually found its way to London, and was sold for
£80,000. The best part of the story is, however, to come. There
was a certain newspaper correspondent in the camp (not Mr
Russell), who depended on his native servant to translate Hindustani names into English. When he heard that a company of the
Ninety-Third had found a gold *tazia* of great value, and that they
had presented the senior lieutenant with the lid of it to enable him
to deposit money to purchase his captaincy, the correspondent
asked his Madrassi servant the English equivalent for *tazia*.
Samuel, perhaps not knowing the English word *tomb*, but knowing
that the *tazia* referred to a funeral, told his master that the English
for *tazia* was *coffin*; so it went the round of the English papers that
among the plunder of Lucknow a certain company of the Ninety-
Third had found a gold coffin, and that they had generously presented the senior lieutenant with the lid of it, which was studded
with diamonds and other precious stones.

As already mentioned, with the exception of the company which
captured the golden *tazia* and the Muharram paraphernalia, the
Ninety-Third got very little loot; and by the time we returned to
the city order was in some measure restored, prize-agents appointed, and guards placed at the different thoroughfares to intercept
camp-followers and other plunderers on their way back to camp,
who were thus made to disgorge their plunder, nominally for the
public good or the benefit of the army. But it was shrewdly sus-
pected by the troops that certain small caskets in battered cases,
which contained the redemption of mortgaged estates in Scotland,

* The name given to the horse used in the celebration of Muharram. [M.E.]

England, and Ireland, and snug fishing and shooting-boxes in every game-haunted and salmon-frequented angle of the world, found their way inside the uniform-cases of even the prize-agents. I could myself name one deeply-encumbered estate which was cleared of mortgage to the tune of £180,000 within two years of the plunder of Lucknow. Before we left Lucknow the plunder accumulated by the prize-agents was estimated at over £600,000 (according to *The Times* of 31st of May, 1858), and within a week it had reached a million and a quarter sterling. What became of it all? Each private soldier who served throughout the relief and capture of Lucknow got prize-money to the value of Rs. 17.8; but the thirty *lakhs* of treasure which were found in the well at Bithur, leaving the plunder of the Nana Sahib's palace out of the calculation, much more than covered that amount.

Many camp-followers and others managed to evade the guards, and cavalry-patrols were put on duty along the different routes on both banks of the Gumti and in the wider thoroughfares of Lucknow.

You will remember I gave it as my opinion that the provost-marshal's cat is the only general which can put a stop to plundering and restore order in times like those I describe, or rather I should say, *which I cannot* describe, because it is impossible to find words to depict the scenes which met one's eyes at every turn in the streets of Lucknow. In and around Hazratgunge, the Imambara, and Kaisarbagh, mad riot and chaos reigned—sights fit only for the Inferno. I had heard the phrase 'drunk with plunder'; I then saw it illustrated in real earnest. Soldiers mad with pillage and wild with excitement, followed by crowds of camp-followers too cowardly to go to the front, but as ravenous as the vultures which followed the army and preyed on the carcases of the slain. I have already said that many of the enemy had to be dislodged from close rooms by throwing in bags of gunpowder with slow-matches fixed to them. When these exploded they set fire to clothing, cotton-padded quilts, and other furniture in the rooms; and the consequence was that in the inner apartments of the palaces there were hundreds of dead bodies half burnt; many wounded were burnt alive with the dead, and the stench from such rooms was horrible! Historians tell us that Charles the Ninth of France, asserted that the smell of a dead enemy was always sweet. If he had experienced the streets of Lucknow in March, 1858, he might have had cause to modify his opinion.

14. FAREWELL TO LUCKNOW

MY company had been posted in a large building and garden near the Mint. Shortly after our arrival an order came for a non-commissioned officer and a guard of selected men to take charge of a house with a harem, or *zenana*, of about eighty women who had been rescued from different harems about the Kaisarbagh—begums of rank and of no rank, dancing girls and household female slaves, some young and others of very doubtful age. Mr MacBean, our adjutant, selected me for the duty, first because he said he knew I would not get drunk and thus overlook my sense of responsibility; and, secondly, because by that time I had picked up a considerable knowledge of colloquial Hindustani, and was thus able to understand natives who could not speak English, and to make myself understood by them. I got about a dozen old soldiers with me, several of whom had been named for the duty by Sir Colin Campbell himself, mostly married men of about twenty years' service. John Ellis, whose wife had acted as laundress for Sir Colin in the Crimea, was one of them, and James Strachan, who was nicknamed 'the Bishop', was another; John M'Donald, the fourth of the name in my company, was a third. They were all old men, tried and true, and, as our adjutant said, Sir Colin had told him that no other corps except the Ninety-Third could be trusted to supply a guard for such a duty. MacBean, along with a staff or civil officer, accompanied the guard to the house, and was very particular in impressing on my attention the fact that the guard was on no pretence whatever to attempt to hold any communication with the begums, except through a shrivelled, parchment-faced, wicked-looking old woman (as I supposed), who, the staff-officer told me, could speak English, and who had been directed to report any shortcomings of the guard, should we not behave ourselves circumspectly. But I must say I had little to fear on that head, for I knew every one of my men could be trusted to be proof against the temptation of begums, gold, or grog, and as for myself, I was then a young non-commissioned officer with a very keen sense of my responsibility.

Shortly after we were installed in our position of trust, and the officers had left us, we discovered several pairs of bright eyes peeping out at us through the partly shattered venetians forming the doors and windows of the house; and the person whom I had taken for a shrivelled old woman came out and entered into conversation with me, at first in Hindustani, but afterwards in very good and grammatical English. I then discovered that what I had mistaken for a crack-voiced old woman was no other than a confidential eunuch of the palace, who told me he had been over thirty years about the court of Lucknow, employed as a sort of private secretary under successive kings, as he was able to read and write English, and could translate the English newspapers, etc., and could also, judging from his villainous appearance, be trusted to strangle a refractory begum or cut the throat of anyone prying too closely into court secrets. He was almost European in complexion, and appeared to me to be more than seventy years of age, but he may have been much younger. He also told me that most of his early life had been spent at the court of Constantinople, and that he had there learned English, and had found this of great use to him at the court of Lucknow, where he had not only kept up the knowledge, but had improved it by reading.

By this time one of the younger begums, or nautch girls (I don't know which), came out to see the guard, and did not appear by any means too bashful. She evidently wished for a closer acquaintance, and I asked my friend to request her to go back to her companions; but this she declined to do, and wanted particularly to know why we were dressed in petticoats, and if we were not part of the Queen of England's regiment of eunuchs, and chaffed me a good deal about my fair hair and youthful appearance. I was twenty-four hours on that guard before the begums were removed by Major Bruce to a house somewhere near the Martinière, and during that twenty-four hours I learned more, through the assistance of the English-speaking eunuch, about the virtues of polygamy and the domestic slavery intrigues, and crimes of the harem than I have learned in all my other years in India. If I dared, I could write a few pages that would give the Government of India and the public of England ten times more light on those cherished institutions than they now possess. The authorities professed to take charge of those caged begums for their own safety, but I don't think many of them were over-thankful for the protection. Major Bruce, with an escort, removed the ladies the next day, and I took leave of my communicative friend and the begums without reluctance, and rejoined my company, glad to be rid of such a dangerous charge.

Except the company which stormed the Durgah, the rest of the Ninety-Third were employed more as guards on our return to the city; but about the 23rd of the month Captain Burroughs and his company were detailed, with some of Brazier's Sikhs, to drive a lot of rebels from some mosques and large buildings which were the last positions held by the enemy. The Ninety-Third had three commanding officers in one day! Lieutenant-Colonel MacDonald and Major Middleton both died within a few hours of each other, and Burroughs at once became senior major and succeeded to the command, the senior colonel, Sir H. Stisted, being in command of a brigade in Bengal. Burroughs was born in India and was sent to France early for his education, at least for the military part of it, and was a cadet of the *Ecole Polytechnique* of Paris. This accounted for his excellent swordsmanship, his thorough knowledge of French, and his foreign accent. Burroughs was an accomplished *maître d'armes*. When he joined the Ninety-Third as an ensign in 1850 he was known as 'Wee Frenchie'. I don't exactly remember his height, I think it was under five feet; but what he wanted in size he made up in pluck and endurance. He served throughout the Crimean War, and was never a day absent. It was he who volunteered to lead the forlorn hope when it was thought the Highland Brigade were to storm the Redan, before it was known that the Russians had evacuated the position. At the relief of Lucknow he was the first *officer* of the regiment to go through the hole in the Secundrabagh, and was immediately attacked by an Oudh Irregular *sowar** armed with *tulwar* and shield, who nearly slashed Burroughs' right ear off before he got properly on his feet. It was the wire frame of his feather bonnet that saved him; the *sowar* got a straight cut at his head, but the sword glanced off the feather bonnet and nearly cut off his right ear. However, Burroughs soon gathered himself together (there was so little of him!) and showed his tall opponent that he had for once met his match in the art of fencing; before many seconds Burroughs' sword had passed through his opponent's throat and out at the back of his neck. Notwithstanding his severe wound, Burroughs fought throughout the capture of the Secundrabagh, with his right ear nearly severed

* Cavalryman. [M.E.]

from his head, and the blood running down over his shoulders to
his gaiters; nor did he go to have his wound dressed till after he
had mustered his company, and reported to the colonel how many
of No. 6 had fallen that morning. Although his men disliked many
of his ways, they were proud of their little captain for his pluck and
good heart. I will relate two instances of this. When promoted,
Captain Burroughs had the misfortune to succeed the most popular
officer in the regiment in the command of his company, namely,
Captain Ewart, and, among other innovations, Burroughs tried to
introduce certain *Polytechnique* ideas new to the Ninety-Third. At
the first morning parade after assuming command of the company,
he wished to satisfy himself that the ears of the men were clean
inside, but being so short, he could not, even on tiptoe, raise
himself high enough to see; he therefore made them come to the
kneeling position, and went along the front rank from left to right,
minutely inspecting the inside of every man's ears! The Ninety-
Third were all tall men in those days, none being under five feet
six inches even in the centre of the rear rank of the battalion companies; and the right-hand man of Burroughs' company was a
stalwart Highlander named Donald MacLean, who could scarcely
speak English and stood about six feet three inches. When Burroughs examined Donald's ears he considered them dirty, and told
the colour-sergeant to put Donald down for three days' extra drill.
Donald, hearing this, at once sprang to his feet from the kneeling
position and, looking down on the little captain with a look of
withering scorn, deliberately said, 'She will take three days' drill
from a man, but not from a monkey!' Of course Donald was at once
marched to the rear-guard a prisoner, and a charge lodged against
him for 'insubordination and insolence to Captain Burroughs at the
time of inspection on morning parade'. When the prisoner was
brought before the colonel he read over the charge, and, turning
to Captain Burroughs, said: 'This is a most serious charge, Captain Burroughs, and against an old soldier like Donald MacLean
who has never been brought up for punishment before. How did it
happen?' Burroughs was ashamed to state the exact words, but
beat about the bush, saying that he had ordered MacLean three
days' drill, and that he refused to submit to the sentence, making
use of most insolent and insubordinate language; but the colonel
could not get him to state the exact words used, and the colour-
sergeant was called as second witness. The colour-sergeant gave a

plain, straightforward account of the ear-inspection; and when he
stated how MacLean had sprung to his feet on hearing the sentence
of three days' drill, and had told the captain, 'She will take three
days' drill from a man, but not from a monkey,' the whole of the
officers present burst into fits of laughter, and even the colonel had
to hold his hand to his mouth. As soon as he could speak he turned
on MacLean, and told him that he deserved to be tried by a court-
martial and so forth, but ended by sentencing him to 'three days'
grog stopped.' The orderly-room hut was then cleared of all except
the colonel, Captain Burroughs, and the adjutant, and no one ever
knew exactly what passed; but there was no repetition of the
kneeling position for ear-inspection on morning parade. I have
already said that Burroughs had a most kindly heart, and for the
next three days after this incident, when the grog bugle sounded,
Donald MacLean was as regularly called to the captain's tent, and
always returned smacking his lips, and emphatically stating that
'The captain was a Highland gentleman after all, and not a French
monkey.' From that day forward, the little captain and the tall
grenadier became the best of friends, and years after, on the evening of the 11th of March, 1858, when the killed and wounded were
collected after the capture of the Begum Kothi in Lucknow, I saw
Captain Burroughs crying like a tender-hearted woman by the side
of a *dooly* in which was stretched the dead body of Donald MacLean,
who, it was said, received his death-wound defending his captain.
I have the authority of the late colour-sergeant of No. 6 company
for the statement that from the date of the death of MacLean,
Captain Burroughs regularly remitted thirty shillings a month,
through the minister of her parish, to Donald's widowed mother.
When an action of this kind became generally known in the regiment, it caused many to look with kindly feelings on most of the
peculiarities of Burroughs.

The other anecdote goes back to Camp Kamara and the spring
of 1856, when the Highland Brigade were lying there half-way
between Balaklava and Sebastopol. As before noticed, Burroughs
was more like a Frenchman than a Highlander; there were many
of his old *Polytechnique* chums in the French Army in the Crimea,
and almost every day he had some visitors from the French camp,
especially after the armistice was proclaimed.

Some time in the spring of 1856 Burroughs had picked up a
Tartar pony and had got a saddle, etc., for it, but he could get no

regular groom. Not being a field-officer he was not entitled to a regulation groom, and not being well liked, none of his company would volunteer for the billet, especially as it formed no excuse for getting off other duties. One of the company had accordingly to be detailed on fatigue duty every day to groom the captain's pony. On a particular day this duty had fallen to a young recruit who had lately joined by draft, a man named Patrick Doolan, a real Paddy of the true Handy Andy type, who had made his way somehow to Glasgow and had there enlisted into the Ninety-Third. This day, as usual, Burroughs had visitors from the French camp, and it was proposed that all should go for a ride, so Patrick Doolan was called to saddle the captain's pony. Doolan had never saddled a pony in his life before, and he put the saddle on with the pommel to the tail and the crupper to the front, and brought the pony thus accoutred to the captain's hut. Every one commenced to laugh, and Burroughs, getting into a white heat, turned on Patrick, saying, 'You fool, you have put the saddle on with the back to the front!' Patrick at once saluted, and, without the least hesitation, replied, 'Shure, sir, you never told me whether you were to ride to Balaklava or Sebastopol.' Burroughs was so tickled with the ready wit of the reply that from that day he took Doolan into his service as soldier-servant, taught him his work, and retained him till March, 1858, when Burroughs had to go on sick leave on account of wounds. Burroughs was one of the last men wounded in the taking of Lucknow. Some days after the Begum Kothi was stormed, he and his company were sent to drive a lot of rebels out of a house near the Kaisarbagh, and, as usual, Burroughs was well in advance of his men. Just as they were entering the place the enemy fired a mine, and the captain was sent about a hundred feet in the air; but being like a cat (in the matter of being difficult to kill, I mean), he fell on his feet on the roof of a thatched hut, and escaped, with his life indeed, but with one of his legs broken in two places below the knee. It was only the skill of our good doctor Munro that saved his leg; but he was sent to England on sick leave, and before he returned I had left the regiment and joined the Commissariat Department.

By the end of March the Ninety-Third returned to camp at the Dilkusha, glad to get out of the city, where we were suffocated by the stench of rotting corpses, and almost devoured with flies by day and mosquitoes by night. The weather was now very hot and altogether uncomfortable, more especially since we were without any means of bathing and could obtain no regular changes of clothing.

By this time numbers of the townspeople had returned to the city and were putting their houses in order, while thousands of *coolies* and low-caste natives were employed clearing dead bodies out of houses and hidden corners, and generally cleaning up the city.

When we repassed the scene of our hard-contested struggle, the Begum's palace—which, I may here remark, was actually a much stronger position than the famous Redan at Sebastopol—we found the inner ditch, that had given us so much trouble to get across, converted into a vast grave, in which the dead had been collected in thousands and then covered by the earth which the enemy had piled up as ramparts. All round Lucknow for miles the country was covered with dead carcases of every kind—human beings, horses, camels, bullocks, and donkeys—and for miles the atmosphere was tainted and the swarms of flies were horrible, a positive torment and a nuisance. The only comfort was that they roosted at night; but at meal-times they were indescribable, and it was impossible to keep them out of our food; our plates of rice would be perfectly black with flies, and it was surprising how we kept such good health, for we had little or no sickness during the siege of Lucknow.

During the few days we remained in camp at the Dilkusha the army was broken up into movable columns, to take the field after the different parties of rebels and to restore order throughout Oudh; for although Lucknow had fallen, the rebellion was not by any means over; the whole of Oudh was still against us, and had to be reconquered. The Forty-Second, Seventy-Ninth, and Ninety-Third (the regiments which composed the famous old Highland Brigade of the Crimea) were once more formed into one brigade, and with a regiment of Punjab Infantry and a strong force of engineers, the Ninth Lancers, a regiment of native cavalry, a strong force of artillery, both light and heavy—in brief, as fine a little army as ever took the field, under the command of General Walpole, with Adrian Hope as brigadier—was detailed for the advance into Rohilkhand for the recapture of Bareilly, where a large army still held together under Khan Bahadur Khan. Every one in the camp expressed surprise that Sir Colin should entrust his favourite Highlanders to Walpole.

On the morning of the 7th of April, 1858, the time had at last arrived when we were to leave Lucknow, and the change was hailed by us with delight. We were glad to get away from the captured city, with its horrible smells and still more horrible sights, and looked forward with positive pleasure to a hot-weather campaign in Rohilkhand. We were to advance on Bareilly by a route parallel with the course of the Ganges, so striking our tents at 2 a.m. we marched through the city along the right bank of the Gumti, past the Musabagh, where our first halt was made, about five miles out of Lucknow, in the midst of fresh fields, away from all the offensive odours and the myriads of flies. One instance will suffice to give my readers some idea of the torment we suffered from these pests. When we struck tents all the flies were roosting in the roofs; when the tents were rolled up the flies got crushed and killed by bushels, and no one who has not seen such a sight would credit the state of the inside of our tents when opened out to be repitched on the new ground. After the tents were pitched and the roofs swept down, the sweepers of each company were called to collect the dead flies and carry them out of the camp. I noted down the quantity of flies carried out of my own tent. The ordinary kitchen-baskets served out to the regimental cooks by the commissariat for carrying bread, rice, etc., will hold about an imperial bushel, and from one tent there were carried out five basketfuls of dead flies. The sight gave one a practical idea of one of the ten plagues of Egypt! Being now rid of the flies we could lie down during the heat of the day, and have a sleep without being tormented.

The defeated army of Lucknow had flocked into Rohilkhand, and a large force was reported to be collected in Bareilly under Khan Bahadur Khan and Prince Firoz Shah. The following is a copy of one of Khan Bahadur Khan's proclamations for the harassment of our advance: 'Do not attempt to meet the regular columns of the infidels, because they are superior to you in discipline and have more guns; but watch their movements; guard all the *ghats* on the rivers; intercept their communications; stop their supplies; cut up their piquets and *daks*; keep constantly hanging about their camps; give them no rest!' These were, no doubt, the correct tactics; it was the old Maratha policy revived. However, nothing came of it, and our advance was unopposed till we reached the jungle fort of Narput Singh, the Rajput chief of Ruiya. I remember the morning

well. I was in the advance-guard under command of a young
officer who had just come out from home as a cadet in the H.E.I.
Company's* service, and there being no Company's regiments for
him, he was attached to the Ninety-Third before we left Lucknow.
His name was Wace, a tall young lad of, I suppose, sixteen or
seventeen years of age. I don't remember him before that morning,
but he was most anxious for a fight, and I recollect that before we
marched off our camping-ground, Brigadier Hope called up young
Mr Wace, and gave him instructions about moving along with
great caution with about a dozen picked men for the leading section
of the advance-guard.

We advanced without opposition till sunrise, and then we came
in sight of an outpost of the enemy about three miles from the fort;
but as soon as they saw us they retired, and word was passed back
to the column. Shortly afterwards instructions came for the
advance-guard to wait for the main column, and I remember young
Mr Wace going up to the brigadier, and asking to be permitted to
lead the assault on the fort, should it come to a fight. At this time
a summons to surrender had been sent to the Raja, but he vouch-
safed no reply, and, as we advanced, a 9-pounder shot was fired at
the head of the column, killing a drummer of the Forty-Second.

The attack on the fort then commenced, without any attempt
being made to reconnoitre the position, and ended in a most severe
loss, Brigadier Hope being among the killed. Lieutenant Wil-
loughby, who commanded the Sikhs—a brother of the officer who
blew up the powder-magazine at Delhi, rather than let it fall into
the hands of the enemy—was also killed; as were Lieutenants
Douglas and Bramley of the Forty-Second, with nearly one
hundred men, Highlanders and Sikhs. Hope was shot from a high
tree inside the fort, and, at the time, it was believed that the man
who shot him was a European.

After we retired from the fort the excitement was so great
among the men of the Forty-Second and Ninety-Third, owing to
the sacrifice of so many officers and men through sheer mismanage-
ment, that if the officers had given the men the least encourage-
ment, I am convinced they would have turned out in a body and
hanged General Walpole. The officers who were killed were all
most popular men; but the great loss sustained by the death of
Adrian Hope positively excited the men to fury. So heated was the

* Honourable East India Company. [M.E.]

Conflict with the Ghazis before Bareilly

feeling on the night the dead were buried, that if any non-commissioned officer had dared to take the lead, the life of General Walpole would not have been worth half an hour's purchase.

After the force retired—for we actually retired!—from Ruiya on the evening of the 15th of April, we encamped about two miles from the place, and a number of our dead were left in the ditch, mostly Forty-Second and Sikhs; and, so far as I am aware, no attempt was made to invest the fort or to keep the enemy in. They took advantage of this to retreat during the night; but this they did leisurely, burning their own dead, and stripping and mutilating those of our force that were abandoned in the ditch. It was reported in the camp that Colonel Haggard of the Ninth Lancers, commanding the cavalry brigade, had proposed to invest the place, but was not allowed to do so by General Walpole, who was said to have acted in such a pig-headed manner that the officers considered him insane. Rumour added that when Colonel Haggard and a squadron of the Lancers went to reconnoitre the place on the morning of the 16th, it was found empty; and that when Colonel Haggard sent an aide-de-camp to report this fact to the general, he had replied, 'Thank God!' appearing glad that Raja Narput Singh and his force had slipped through his fingers after beating back the best-equipped movable column in India. These reports gaining currency in the camp made the general still more unpopular, because, in addition to his incapability as an officer, the men put him down as a coward.

During the day the mutilated bodies of our men were recovered from the ditch. The Sikhs burnt theirs, while a large fatigue party of the Forty-Second and Ninety-Third was employed digging one long grave in a *tope* of trees not far from the camp. About four o'clock in the afternoon the funeral took place, Brigadier Hope and the officers on the right, wrapped in their tartan plaids, the non-commissioned officers and the privates on their left, each sewn up in a blanket. The Rev Mr Cowie, whom we of the Ninety-Third had nicknamed 'the Fighting Padre', and the Rev Mr Ross, chaplain of the Forty-Second, conducted the service, Mr Ross reading the ninetieth Psalm and Mr Cowie the rest of the service. The pipers of the Forty-Second and Ninety-Third, with muffled drums, played *The Flowers of the Forest* as a dead march. In all my experience in the army or out of it I never witnessed such intense grief, both among officers and men, as was expressed at this funeral.

Many of all ranks sobbed like tender-hearted women. I especially remember our surgeon, 'kind-hearted Billy Munro' as the men called him; also Lieutenants Archie Butter and Dick Cunningham, who were aides-de-camp to Adrian Hope. Cunningham had rejoined the regiment after recovery from his wounds in October, 1857, but they had left him too lame to march, and he was a supernumerary aide-de-camp to Brigadier Hope; he and Butter were both alongside the brigadier, I believe, when he was struck down by the renegade ruffian.

We halted during the 17th, and strong fatigue-parties were employed with the engineers destroying the fort by blowing up the gateways. The place was ever after known in the Ninety-Third as 'Walpole's Castle'. On the 18th we marched, and on the 22nd we came upon the retreating rebels at a place called Sirsa, on the Ramgunga. The Ninth Lancers and Horse-Artillery and two companies of the Ninety-Third crossed the Ramgunga by a ford and intercepted the retreat of a large number of the enemy, who were escaping by a bridge of boats, the material for which the country people had collected for them. But their retreat was now completely cut off, and about three hundred of them were reported either killed or drowned in the Ramgunga.

About 3 p.m. a tremendous sandstorm, with thunder, and rain in torrents, came on. The Ramgunga became so swollen that it was impossible for the detachment of the Ninety-Third to recross, and they bivouacked in a deserted village on the opposite side, without tents, the officers hailing across that they could make themselves very comfortable for the night if they could only get some tea and sugar, as the men had biscuits, and they had secured a quantity of flour and some goats in the village. But the boats which the enemy had collected had all broken adrift, and there was apparently no possibility of sending anything across to our comrades. This dilemma evoked an act of real cool pluck on the part of our commissariat *gomashta*,* babu Hira Lal Chatterjee, whom I have before mentioned in reference to the plunder of a cartload of biscuits on the retreat from Lucknow. By this time Hira Lal had become better acquainted with the 'wild Highlanders', and was even ready to risk his life to carry a ration of tea and sugar to them. This he made into a bundle, which he tied on the crown of his head, and although several of the officers tried to dissuade him from the attempt, he

* Native assistant in charge of stores.

tightened his *chudder** round his waist, and declaring that he had often swum the Hugli, and that the Ramgunga should not deprive the officers and men of a detachment of his regiment of their tea, he plunged into the river, and safely reached the other side with his precious freight on his head! This little incident was never forgotten in the regiment so long as Hira Lal remained the commissariat *gomashta* of the Ninety-Third.

Among the enemy killed that day were several wearing uniforms stripped from the dead of the Forty-Second in the ditch of Ruiya; so, of course, we concluded that this was Narput Singh's force, and the defeat and capture of its guns in some measure, I have no doubt, re-established General Walpole in the good opinion of the authorities, but not much in that of the force under his command.

Nothing else of consequence occurred till about the 27th of April, when our force rejoined the Commander-in-Chief's column, which had advanced *via* Fatehgarh, and we heard that Sir William Peel† had died of smallpox at Cawnpore on his way to Calcutta. The news went through the camp from regiment to regiment, and caused almost as much sorrow in the Ninety-Third as the death of poor Adrian Hope.

---

* A wrapper worn by Bengali men and up-country women.
† Captain Peel of the Naval Brigade. [M.E.]

15. THE END OF THE MUTINY

THE heat was now very oppressive, and we had many men struck down by the sun every day. We reached Shahjahanpur on the 30th of April, and found that every building in the cantonments fit for sheltering European troops had been destroyed by order of the Nana Sahib, who, however, did not himself wait for our arrival. Strange to say, the bridge of boats across the Ramgunga was not destroyed, and some of the buildings in the jail, and the wall round it, were still standing. Colonel Hale and a wing of the Eighty-Second were left here with some guns, to make the best of their position in the jail, which partly dominated the city. The Shahjahanpur distillery was mostly destroyed, but the native distillers had been working it, and there was a large quantity of rum still in the vats, which was found to be good and was consequently annexed by the commissariat.

On the 2nd of May we left Shahjahanpur *en route* for Bareilly, and on the next day reached Fatehgunge. Every village was totally deserted, but no plundering was allowed, and any camp-followers found marauding were soon tied up by the provost-marshal's staff. Proclamations were sent everywhere for the people to remain in their villages, but without any effect. Two days later we reached Faridpur, which we also found deserted, but with evident signs that the enemy were near; and our bazaars were full of reports of the great strength of the army of Khan Bahadur Khan and Firoz Shah. The usual estimate was thirty thousand infantry, twenty-five thousand cavalry, and about three hundred guns, among which was said to be a famous black battery that had beaten the European artillery at ball-practice a few months before they mutinied at Meerut. The left wing of the Ninety-Third was thrown out, with a squadron of the Lancers and Captain Tombs' battery, as the advance piquet. As darkness set in we could see the fires of the enemy's outposts, their patrol advancing quite close to our sentries during the night, but making no attack.

About 2 a.m. on the 5th of May, according to Sir Colin's usual plan, three days' rations were served out, and the whole force was under arms and slowly advancing before daylight. By sunrise we could see the enemy drawn up on the plain some five miles from Bareilly, in front of what had been the native lines; but as we advanced, they retired. By noon we had crossed the *nullah* [ravine] in front of the old cantonments, and, except by sending round-shot among us at long distances, which did not do much harm, the enemy did not dispute our advance. We were halted in the middle of a bare, sandy plain, and we of the rank and file then got to understand why the enemy were apparently in some confusion; we could hear the guns of Brigadier Jones ('Jones the Avenger' as he was called) hammering at them on the other side. The Ninety-Third formed the extreme right of the front line of infantry with a squadron of the Lancers and Tombs' battery of horse-artillery. The heat was intense, and when about two o'clock a movement in the mango groves in our front caused the order to stand to arms, it attained such a pitch that the barrels of our rifles could not be touched by our bare hands!

The Sikhs and our light company advanced in skirmishing order, when some seven to eight hundred matchlock-men opened fire on them, and all at once a most furious charge was made by a body of about three hundred and sixty Rohilla Ghazis, who rushed out, shouting '*Bismillah! Allah! Allah! Din! Din!*' Sir Colin was close by, and called out 'Ghazis, Ghazis! Close up the ranks! Bayonet them as they come on.' However, they inclined to our left, and only a few came on to the Ninety-Third, and these were mostly bayoneted by the light company which was extended in front of the line. The main body rushed on the centre of the Forty-Second; but as soon as he saw them change their direction Sir Colin galloped on, shouting out, 'Close up, Forty-Second! Bayonet them as they come on!' But that was not so easily done; the Ghazis charged in blind fury, with their round shields on their left arms, their bodies bent low, waving their *tulwars* over their heads, throwing themselves under the bayonets, and cutting at the men's legs. Colonel Cameron, of the Forty-Second, was pulled from his horse by a Ghazi, who leaped up and seized him by the collar while he was engaged with another on the opposite side; but his life was saved by Colour-Sergeant Gardener, who seized one of the enemy's *tulwars*, and rushing to the colonel's assistance cut off the Ghazi's head. General Walpole was also pulled off his horse and received two sword-cuts, but was rescued by the bayonets of the Forty-Second. The struggle was short, but every one of the Ghazis was killed. None attempted to escape; they had evidently come on to kill or be killed, and a hundred and thirty-three lay in one circle right in front of the colours of the Forty-Second.

The Commander-in-Chief himself saw one of the Ghazis, who had broken through the line, lying down, shamming dead. Sir Colin caught the glance of his eye, saw through the ruse, and called to one of the Forty-Second, 'Bayonet that man!' But the Ghazi was enveloped in a thick quilted tunic of green silk, through which the blunt Enfield bayonet would not pass, and the Highlander was in danger of being cut down, when a Sikh officer of the Fourth Punjabis rushed to his assistance, and took the Ghazi's head clean off with one sweep of his keen *tulwar*. These Ghazis, with a very few exceptions, were grey-bearded men of the Rohilla race, clad in green, with green turbans and *cummerbands*, round shields on the left arm, and curved *tulwars* that would split a hair. They only succeeded in wounding about twenty men—they threw themselves so wildly on the bayonets of the Forty-Second! One of them, an exception to the majority, was quite a youth, and having got separated from the rest challenged the whole of the line to come out and fight him. He then rushed at Mr Joiner, the quartermaster of the Ninety-Third, firing his carbine, but missing. Mr Joiner returned the fire with his revolver, and the Ghazi then threw away his carbine and rushed at Joiner with his *tulwar*. Some of the light company tried to take the youngster prisoner, but it was no use; he cut at every one so madly, that they had to bayonet him.

The commotion caused by this attack was barely over, when word was passed that the enemy were concentrating in front for another rush, and the order was given for the spare ammunition to be brought to the front. I was detached with about a dozen men of No. 7 company to find the ammunition-guard, and bring our ammunition in rear of the line. Just as I reached the ammunition-camels, a large force of the rebel cavalry, led by Firoz Shah in person, swept round the flank and among the baggage, cutting down camels, camel-drivers, and camp-followers in all directions. My detachment united with the ammunition guard and defended ourselves, shooting down a number of the enemy's cavalry. I remember the Rev Mr Ross, chaplain of the Forty-Second, running for his life, dodging round camels and bullocks with a rebel *sowar* after him, till, seeing our detachment, he rushed to us for protection, calling out, 'Ninety-Third, shoot that impertinent fellow!'

Bob Johnston, of my company, shot him down. Mr Ross had no sword nor revolver, and not even a stick with which to defend himself. Moral—when in the field, *padres*, carry a good revolver! About the same time as Mr Ross gained our protection, we saw Mr Russell, of *The Times*, who was ill and unable to walk from the kick of a horse, trying to escape on horseback. He had got out of his *dooly*, undressed and bareheaded as he was, and leaped into the saddle, as the groom had been leading his horse near him. Several of the enemy's cavalry were dodging through the camels to get at him. We turned our rifles on them, and I shot down the one nearest to Mr Russell, just as he had cut down an intervening camel-driver and was making for 'Our Special Correspondent'; in fact, his *tulwar* was actually lifted to swoop down on Mr Russell's bare head when my bullet put a stop to his proceedings. I saw Mr Russell tumble from his saddle at the same instant as the cavalryman fell, and I got a rare fright, for I thought my bullet must have struck both. However, I rushed to where Mr Russell had fallen, and I then saw from the position of the slain cavalryman that my bullet had found its proper billet, and that Mr Russell was down with sunstroke, the blood flowing freely from his nose. There was no time to lose. Our Multani Irregulars were after the enemy, and I had to hasten to the line with the spare ammunition; but before I left Mr Russell to his fate, I called some of the Forty-Second baggage-guards to put him into his *dooly* and take him to their doctor, while I hastened back to the line and reported the occurrence to Captain Dawson. Next morning I was glad to hear that Mr Russell was still alive, and likely to get over his stroke.

After this charge of the rebel cavalry we were advanced; but the thunder of Jones' attack on the other side of the city evidently disconcerted the enemy, and they made off to the right of our line, while large numbers of Ghazis concentrated themselves in the main buildings of the city. We suffered more from the sun than from the enemy; and after we advanced into the shelter of a large mango grove we were nearly eaten alive by swarms of small green insects, which invaded our bare legs in thousands, till we were glad to leave the shelter of the mango trees and take to the open plain again. As night drew on the cantonments were secured, the baggage was collected, and we bivouacked on the plain, strong piquets being thrown out. My company was posted in a small field of onions near a well with a Persian wheel for lifting the water. We supped off the biscuits in our haversacks, raw onions, and the cool water drawn from well, and then went off to sleep. I wish I might always sleep as soundly as I did that night after my supper of raw onions and dry biscuits!

On the 6th May the troops were under arms, and advanced on the city of Bareilly. But little opposition was offered, except from one large house on the outskirts of the town, in which a body of about fifty Rohilla Ghazis had barricaded themselves, and a company (I think it was No. 6 of the Ninety-Third) was sent to storm the house, after several shells had been pitched into it. This was done without much loss, except of one man; I now forget his name, but think it was William MacDonald. He rushed into a room full of Ghazis, who, before his comrades could get to his assistance, had cut him into sixteen pieces with their sharp *tulwars!* As the natives said, he was cut into annas. But the house was taken, and the whole of the Ghazis slain, with only the loss of this one man killed and about half a dozen wounded.

While this house was being stormed the townspeople sent a deputation of submission to the Commander-in-Chief, and by ten o'clock we had pitched our camp near the ruins of the church which had been destroyed twelve months before. Khan Bahadur Khan and the Nana Sahib were reported to have fled in the direction of the Nepal foothills, while Firoz Shah, with a force of cavalry and guns, had gone back to attack Shahjahanpur.

About midday on the 6th a frightful accident happened, by which a large number of camp-followers and cattle belonging to the ordnance-park were killed. Whether for concealment or by design (it was never known which) the enemy had left a very large quantity of gunpowder and loaded shells in a dry well under a huge tree in the centre of the old cantonment. The well had been filled to the very mouth with powder and shells, and then covered with a thin layer of dry sand. A large number of ordnance *khalasies,* * bullock-drivers, and *dooly*-bearers had congregated under the tree to cook their midday meal, lighting their fires right on the top of this powder-magazine, when it suddenly exploded with a most terrific report, shaking the ground for miles, making the tent-pegs fly out of the hard earth, and throwing down tents more than a mile from the spot. I was lying down in a tent at the time, and the concussion was so great that I felt as if lifted clear off the ground.

* Tent-pitchers.

The tent-pegs flew out all round, and down came the tents, before the men, many of whom were asleep, had time to get clear of the canvas. By the time we got our arms free of the tents, bugles were sounding the assembly in all directions, and staff-officers galloping over the plain to ascertain what had happened. The spot where the accident had occurred was easily found. The powder having been in a deep well, it acted like a huge mortar, fired perpendicularly; an immense cloud of black smoke was sent up in a vertical column at least a thousand yards high, and thousands of shells were bursting in it, the fragments flying all round in a circle of several hundred yards. As the place was not far from the ammunition-park, the first idea was that the enemy had succeeded in blowing up the ammunition; but those who had ever witnessed a similar accident could see that, whatever had happened, the concussion was too great to be caused by only one or two wagon-loads of powder. From the appearance of the column of smoke and the shells bursting in it, as if shot out of a huge mortar, it was evident that the accident was confined to one small spot, and the belief became general that the enemy had exploded an enormous mine. But after some time the truth became known, the troops were dispersed, and the tents repitched. This explosion was followed in the afternoon by a most terrific thunderstorm and heavy rain, which nearly washed away the camp. The storm came on as the non-commissioned officers of the Ninety-Third and No. 2 Company were falling in to bury Colour-Sergeant Mackie, who had been knocked down by the sun the day before and had died that forenoon. Just when we were lowering the body into the grave, there was a crash of thunder almost as loud as the explosion of the powder-mine. The ground becoming soaked with rain, the tent-pegs and many tents were again thrown down by the force of the hurricane; and as everything we had became soaked, we passed a most uncomfortable night.

On the morning of the 7th of May we heard that Colonel Hale and the wing of the Eighty-Second left in the jail at Shahjahanpur had been attacked by Firoz Shah and the Nana Sahib, and were sore pushed to defend themselves. A brigade, consisting of the Sixtieth Rifles, Seventy-Ninth Highlanders, several native regiments, the Ninth Lancers, and some batteries of artillery, under Brigadier John Jones ('the Avenger') was at once started back for the relief of Shahjahanpur—rather a gloomy outlook for the hot

weather of 1858! While this brigade was starting, the remainder
of the force which was to hold Bareilly for the hot season, consisting of the Forty-Second, Seventy-Eighth, and Ninety-Third,
shifted camp to the sandy plain near where Bareilly railway station
now stands, hard by the little fort in the centre of the plain. There
we remained in tents during the whole of May, large working
parties being formed every morning to assist the engineers to get
what shelter was possible ready for the hottest months. The district
jail was arranged as barracks for the Ninety-Third, and we moved
into them on the 1st of June. The Forty-Second got the old court-
house buildings with a new thatch roof; and the Seventy-Eighth
had the Bareilly College. There we remained till October, 1858.

We remained in Bareilly from May till October in comparative
peace. We had one or two false alarms, and a wing of the Forty-
Second, with some cavalry and artillery, went out about the
beginning of June to disperse a body of rebels who were threatening an attack on Muradabad.

About the end of September the weather was comparatively
cool. Many people had returned from Naini Tal to look after their
wrecked property. General Colin Troup with the Sixty-Sixth
Regiment of Gurkhas had come down from Kumaon, and soldiers'
sports were got up for the amusement of the troops and visitors.
Among the latter was the loyal Raja of Rampur, who presented a
thousand rupees for prizes for the games and five thousand for a
dinner to all the troops in the garrison. At these games the Ninety-
Third carried off all the first prizes for putting the shot, throwing
the hammer, and tossing the caber. Our best athlete was a man
named George Bell, of the grenadier company, the most powerful
man in the British army. Before the regiment left England, Bell
had beaten all comers at all the athletic games throughout Scotland.
He stood about six feet four inches, and was built in proportion,
most remarkably active for his size both in running and leaping,
and also renowned for feats of strength. There was a young lad of
the band named Murdoch MacKay, the smallest boy in the regiment, but a splendid dancer; and the two, 'the giant and the pigmy',
as they were called, attended all the athletic games throughout
Scotland from Edinburgh to Inverness, always returning covered
with medals. I mention all this because the Bareilly sports proved
the last to poor George Bell. An enormous caber having been cut,
and all the leading men (among them some very powerful artillery-

men) of the brigade had tried to toss it and failed. The brigadier then ordered three feet to be cut from it, expressing his opinion that there was not a man in the British army who could toss it. On this George Bell stepped into the arena, and said he would take a turn at it before it was cut; he put the huge caber on his shoulders, balanced it, and tossed it clean over. While the caber was being cut for the others, Bell ran in a hundred yards' race, which he also won; but he came in with his mouth full of blood. He had, through over-exertion, burst a blood-vessel in his lungs. He slowly bled to death and died about a fortnight after we left Bareilly. Bell was considered an ornament to, and the pride of, the regiment, and his death was mourned by every officer and man in it, and by none more than by our popular doctor, Billy Munro, who did everything that a physician could do to try and stop the bleeding; but without success. Bell gradually sank till he died.

We left Bareilly on the 10th of October, and marched to Shah-jahanpur, where we were joined by a battalion of the Sixtieth Rifles, the Sixty-Sixth Gurkhas, some of the Sixth Carabineers, Tombs' troop of horse-artillery, and a small train of heavy guns and mortars. On the 17th of October we had our first brush with the enemy at the village of Posgaon, about twenty miles from Shah-jahanpur. Here they were strong in cavalry, and tried the Bareilly game of getting round the flanks and cutting up our camp-followers. But a number of them got hemmed in between the ammunition-guard and the main line, and Cureton's Multani cavalry, coming round on them from both flanks, cut down about fifty of them, capturing their horses. In the midst of this scrim-mage two of the enemy, getting among the baggage-guard, were taken for two of our native cavalry, till at length they separated from the main body and got alongside of a man who was some distance away. One of them called to the poor fellow to look in another direction, when the second one cut his head clean off, leaped from his horse, and, lifting the head, sprang into his saddle and was off like the wind! Many rifle-bullets were sent after him, but he got clear away, carrying the head with him.

The next encounter we had was at Russoolpur, and then at Nowrangabad, where the Queen's proclamation, transferring the government from the Company to the Crown, was read. After this all our tents were sent into Mahomdi, and we took to the jungles without tents or baggage, merely a greatcoat and a blanket; and

thus we remained till after the taking of Maithauli. We then
returned to Sitapur, where we got our tents again the day before
Christmas, 1858; and by the new year we were on the banks of the
Gogra, miles from any village. The river swarmed with alligators
of enormous size, and the jungles with wild pig and every variety
of game, and scarcely a day passed without our seeing tigers,
wolves, and hyaenas. But by this time fighting was over. We
remained in those jungles across the Gogra, in sight of the Nepal
hills, till about the end of February, by which time thousands of
the rebels had tendered their submission and returned to their
homes. The Ninety-Third then got the route for Subathu, in the
Himalayas near Simla. Leaving the jungles of Oudh, we marched
via Shahjahanpur, Bareilly, Muradabad, and thence by the foot of
the hills till we came into civilised regions at Saharunpur; thence
to Umballa, reaching Subathu about the middle of April with our
clothes completely in rags. We had received no new clothing since
we had arrived in India, and our kilts were torn into ribbons. But
the men were in splendid condition, and could have marched thirty
miles a day without feeling fatigued, if our baggage-animals could
have kept up with us. On our march out from Kalka, the Commander-in-Chief passed us on his way to Simla.

This ended the work of the old Ninety-Third Sutherland
Highlanders in the Mutiny.

INDEX

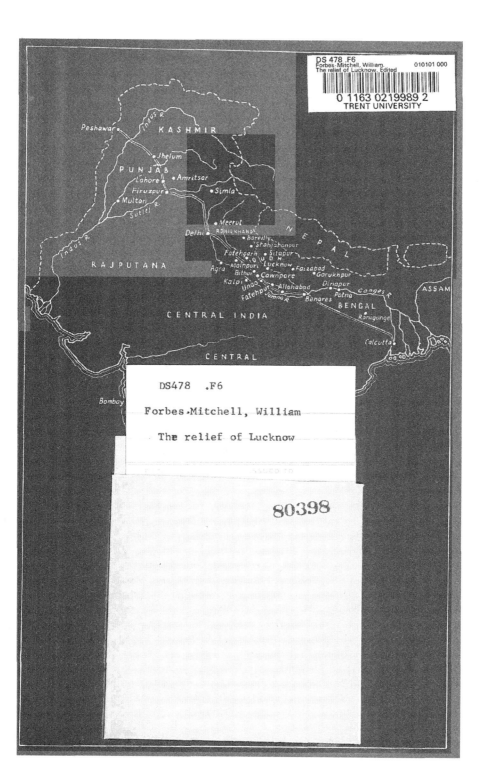

CPSIA information can be obtained
at www.ICGtesting.com
Printed in the USA
BVHW052352080223
658190BV00005B/143